MISSION ACCOMPLISHED

Other Fighting Four Books

MISSION ACCOMPLISHED

by

A. R. CHANNEL

THE CHILDREN'S PRESS

LONDON AND GLASGOW

First printed 1964

CONTENTS

CHAPTER ONE

UNWITTING TRAITOR

FOURTEEN-YEAR-OLD Michaelovitch had been waiting by the rabbit burrow for half an hour, his noose set. In that time he had scarcely moved a muscle. If he could catch a rabbit it would be a triumph, and, made into soup, would be welcomed with shrieks of joy in the cave full of refugees up the hill. He had his ear to the ground, waiting for some slight sound to tell him that the rabbit was getting ready to come out, when he saw the man who was to alter everything.

Michaelovitch frowned. It was strange to see a man alone in these hills. The Germans never moved out except in strong patrols. Peasants kept near their houses. The Partisans—the Yugoslav Resistance movement—only moved at night. If they were caught, it was death with their backs against a wall.

This man seemed to be in trouble. He moved slowly, stumbling often, and sometimes even dropping face down, to lie for a minute or more without movement. That was suspicious, and made Michaelovitch shrink back to the shelter of a rocky outcrop. He did not wish to be seen either. Yet, scan the hills how he would, he could see no one but this man.

Gradually the man drew nearer, and when he was within two hundred yards the keen-eyed youngster picked out something which he thought he recognised.

There was something red on the man's cap. Could it be the red, five-pointed star of the Yugoslav Resistance movement?

Michaelovitch, moving with the cunning of an animal, crept down the hillside until he was near enough to see for certain that the splash of red was indeed a five-pointed star. Hesitating no longer he broke cover and raced down, and was in time to ease the man to the ground as once again he seemed about to fall flat.

"Comrade . . . comrade," Michaelovitch urged, trying to turn the man over. "Are you hurt? What is the matter? I am a friend."

It was not easy to turn the man over, for he was heavily built, and seemed to have drifted off into unconsciousness. What was more, though Michaelovitch was as tough as any youngster could be who had been on the run since the Germans and Italians had occupied Yugoslavia, he was thin from continued underfeeding.

When he did lever the man over, so that he lay on his back, the reason for his strange behaviour, stumbling and falling, became apparent. He had been wounded, not once but three times.

Making him as comfortable as he could, Michaelovitch turned and went up the hillside. He was anxious to bring help, but that did not make him forget caution. He went from one boulder to another, one stunted shrub to another, until he finally reached the mouth of a cave. By then he was gasping for breath, and his entry into the semi-darkness of the big cave produced something like panic.

There were about a hundred children in the cave,

boys and girls, ranging in age from five years to eleven or twelve. In addition there were six women. They were kneeling on the ground, watching a thin soup come to the boil on a small fire.

Two of the women wore big German automatic pistols strapped at their waists, and at the commotion which Michaelovitch's entry caused, these women grabbed for their weapons at once.

"No . . . no. It is all right," Michaelovitch panted. "No danger. I have found a man. A wounded comrade. Down the hill," and he poured out his story. While he was getting back his breath, one of the women filled a wine bottle with water which was welling out of a crack at the far end of the cave. Then, moving as cautiously as possible, for in these wild hills any movement might attract the attention of an unseen watcher, they went down the hill.

Twenty minutes later they carried the wounded man into the cave. He was still unconscious and it was half an hour later before he opened his eyes. He seemed to know that he was dying, and calling on the last ounce of his strength he tapped his belt as he croaked, "A message . . . from a British officer. It must go to Georgi the Black. You understand . . . to Georgi the Black, at once."

Somehow he kept conscious until they had found a cunningly made slit in his belt and brought out a piece of cigarette paper. Then, as he realised his message had been found, his eyes closed and he sank back. They covered him with a ragged sheet. He was one more patriotic Partisan who had given his life for Yugoslavia.

Trici, the eldest of the six women, and the leader, took the flimsy little square of cigarette paper to the cave entrance and read the message. It was brief, but it brought the light of hope to their eyes and the women exchanged swift glances. From the depths of despair they were lifted in a moment to the thought that they might yet win through. The message read:

"Guns, ammunition, explosives and food, with men, will land opposite Cipili on the 28th. Flash a light three times at five-second intervals. The answer is a long, green flash. You will give the British soldiers every assistance."

There was no signature, but no one doubted that it had come from one of the British army officers who had been parachuted into Yugoslavia to help the resistance movement to sabotage the German war effort.

"Food!" One of the women murmured, and made the word sound like a glass of the finest wine. "Just think . . . real food, if this is true."

They all looked back into the cave. The children, who had been playing until the injured man was carried in, were now standing in little groups, whispering or just staring silently at the still form.

There were almost a hundred children, and all of them were homeless, some of them orphans. Those whose parents were not dead had been left to fend for themselves when their villages had been the scene of a battle, and men and women carried away, accused of helping the Partisans.

They were all thin and underfed. Most of them wore the raggedest of clothes, and the six women were now almost at their wits' end to provide even a thin broth for them.

"Somebody must take this message into Cipili," Trici said. "There is a Partisan movement there. They may know where Georgi the Black can be found. If we . . ."

"I shall take it," Michaelovitch insisted, holding his hand out for the piece of paper. "If this ship comes, there might be room to take us all across to Italy. If it is true that the Allies are fighting in Italy now."

"The Allies are in Italy," one of the women agreed, but she was frowning as she added: "But we cannot let you go, Michaelovitch. Who is there to find food for us if you go? You know we are almost starving . . . and no one can steal like you."

There was a moment or so of silence, then Trici held out the paper.

"You must go," she said. "If anyone can find Georgi the Black it is surely you. You have stolen so often from the German patrols that I think sometimes you must have a special cloak of invisibility to shield you. One thing . . . this message must not fall into the hands of the enemy. It would be terrible, an awful betrayal if the Germans found out, and were waiting for these brave men when they tried to get ashore."

"I will swallow the paper if I am caught," Michaelovitch promised, and with a little smile. "After all, there is not much of it, is there?"

For the rest of the day they waited impatiently. Cipili was a small village, and only a few miles away; but it was on a road, and German patrols passed through it often enough on their way to the seaside resort of Cavtat, a few miles up the coast. Only a fool would try to find a Partisan in Cipili in broad daylight.

When he did start across the dusk-shrouded hills, Michaelovitch had committed the short message to memory, so that if he did have to destroy the paper, he would still be able to repeat every word of it when he found Georgi the Black.

Cipili was in complete darkness; not that there was a black-out for fear of bombing. People did not show a light in case the Germans came through and were tempted to knock on the door.

From house to house Michaelovitch went, quiet as a hunting cat. There was no sound anywhere, and he was beginning to despair when he caught sight of a chink of light ahead. It came from a badly-curtained window, and making sure that his precious cigarette paper "letter" was in its hiding place, he was creeping nearer to the light when a shadow swept out from a doorway. An expert hand went across the boy's face, cutting off his gasp of fear. Another hand went round his chest, pinning his arms to his side.

Only when he realised his prisoner was no more than a boy, did the unknown relax. He whipped Michaelovitch off his feet, tucked him under an arm, and walked along towards the chink of light. As the man kicked twice at a door Michaelovitch managed to get his fingers to his "letter." He flicked it out of its hiding place and it drifted on the windless air to the ground.

The light inside the small house was hidden under a box before the door was opened, and only brought out again when the door was shut. Michaelovitch stood blinking in the yellow light of an oil lamp, blinking and staring about at some twenty men.

They were a rough-looking crowd. Some of them lay on benches, snoring. Others were sleeping on the floor. There were rifles and tommy-guns, German, Italian and Greek, stacked in corners; while almost every man seemed to have a big automatic pistol strapped at his waist.

The thing which reassured Michaelovitch were the red stars which adorned the caps he could see hanging from nails knocked into the peeling plaster on the walls. They were the signs used by the real Partisans, the men who supported Marshal Tito. He heaved a sigh of relief, then faced the man seated at a rude table with a grin, saying:

"I would speak with Georgi the Black. I have a message for him from a British army officer. It was to be delivered to the Partisan Leader in Cipili, named Georgi the Black. Is he here?"

"You are a bold young cockerel," the man at the table growled, and shot a quick glance at two other men sitting by a tiny stove. "If you were a German, I would not admit to being Georgi, since that would mean a firing squad."

"Then you are Georgi?" Michaelovitch could hardly conceal his joy. A few minutes earlier he had wondered if he would find any Partisans at all, Cipili had seemed so dead.

"I am Georgi," the man at the table agreed, holding out his hand. "Now, where is this message?"

"I . . . I haven't got it," Michaelovitch had to admit, adding quickly. "I can repeat it word for word."

"Word for word, that's no use," was the angry retort. "Anybody can think up a message."

"Then I can tell you where the message is," Michaelovitch said hastily, and told how he had dropped it on the ground, in case his captor was not a Partisan.

"A-ah, a clever boy, eh," the big man said, rising and clapping an approving hand on the youngster's shoulders. "Well, we'll look. Peti, bring the lamp."

With the aid of the lamp it took them no more than a moment or so to find the thin sheet of paper, for it lay where it had fallen. Indoors again, and now with the men who had been sleeping crowding round, anxious to know what was happening, the message was read out. It was short, but perfectly plain and brought grins of delight to every face:

"Guns, ammunition, explosives and food, with men, will land opposite Cipili on the 28th. Flash a light three times at five-second intervals. The answer is a long green flash. You will give the British soldiers every assistance."

There followed a few moments of silence while Michaelovitch looked anxiously at the man he thought was Georgi the Black. Then he asked:

"Do you think some food could be spared for us? There are over a hundred women and children, starving in a cave in the hills. They must have food."

The tall man rubbed at his unshaven chin for a moment, then grinned. He nodded as he slapped a hand on the back of a companion, winking at him as he said:

"You have nothing to fear, boy. There will be plenty for you. Much more than you can eat. Now, go and rest. Are you hungry?"

"I have been hungry for years," Michaelovitch replied, and amid a chorus of laughs was hurried into a small back room where he was given some stale bread, a piece of cold, undercooked sheep, and a glass of wine to wash the meal down with.

In the larger room the men crowded closer to their leader as he resumed his seat at the table and lit a cigarette. One of the men asked:

"Dare we risk this, Dravadavitch? We are short of ammunition. If there was a fight . . . it might mean death for the lot of us."

"You had better remember to call me Georgi," the big man said, grinning. "Yes, we can risk it. After all, *we* have the message. We know Georgi the Black can't interfere, because he and his men are either dead or prisoners. We know the Germans ambushed them. We can take everything these Britishers put ashore . . . then shoot them. They won't be expecting an ambush. What could be simpler? We just get hold of the stuff, and at the first opportunity, shoot the British down like the dogs they are."

"And what about the boy?" the speaker was darker skinned than the others, and wore the uniform of an Italian soldier. "Is it not better to get rid of him now? You never can tell with boys. If he suspected anything he might run away . . ."

"Giuseppe, he will *not* run away," Dravadavitch assured him, grinning hugely. "I know this boy. I know his father. A man who spent some time in

America. He speaks English, and I think the boy speaks English too. I shall take the boy with me when we go to meet the landing party. What could look more innocent than for a boy to be with us? Where children are concerned the English are fools."

"It may be all right," Giuseppe agreed reluctantly, "but everyone must be sure to remember to call you Georgi, and not by your real name of Dravadavitch."

"I shall see to that," Dravadavitch said grimly. "We shall leave just before dawn, then we can be on the coast in good time. It is the 27th to-morrow, and I never was a man for keeping friends waiting," he winked again, at which his four lieutenants grinned and clapped one another on the shoulders. It looked as if they were in luck's way, just when supplies of ammunition were running short.

They left just before dawn, unseen and unheard. Michaelovitch, who knew the country as well as he knew his own face, acted as guide. It was hard, rough going, but he was able to take them to the coast without once being sighted by anyone.

They waited for the night of the 28th, and then, just before midnight Dravadavitch, whom young Michaelovitch thought was Georgi the Black, flashed a light in the direction of the sea. It was answered at once by a pin-point of bright green.

CHAPTER TWO

YUGOSLAV LANDING

OUT AT SEA, with no light showing save the pale green glow of the compass light, an Italian fishing schooner lurched and wallowed her way nearer the coast. She was an old, wooden vessel, recently fitted with a 70-horse-power British-built diesel; an engine which hustled her through the choppy seas at an uncomfortable nine knots.

Braced against the front of the wheel-house, two figures swathed in dripping oilskins swayed uneasily to the bucking and rolling of their unwieldly craft. Each time the blunt bows cut a wave a sheet of spray went hissing almost down to the stern; the two men hunched their shoulders, but neither took his gaze off the seas ahead.

"I don't like this, Sergeant Harris," one of the men said. "I've got a feeling we are getting far too close to the coast, and you know what the Yugoslav coastline is like. There are supposed to be over a thousand islands dotted about . . . rocky ones."

"I didn't know that, sir," Sergeant Ted Harris said respectfully, "but it isn't very late, yet, is it? Maybe they haven't arrived. Or maybe they think we'll not come until after midnight."

"If that E-boat would clear off I'd feel happier," Major D'Arcy growled, and turned to focus his powerful night glasses on a thin, wavering beam of light which kept coming and going, suggesting there was a vessel somewhere over the horizon scouring the seas for something. "I hope they haven't been tipped off that we are coming. We'd be a sitting duck for an E-boat."

"Yessir," and Sergeant Ted Harris resumed his staring at the blackness ahead.

A few minutes later there came five quick flashes of white light from the unseen coastline. They were high up, suggesting someone on a hill.

"That's it, sir," Ted Harris said eagerly. "Five flashes, as per the signal arranged. Shall I warn the men to stand by?"

"Yes," Major D'Arcy agreed, knocking on the wheelhouse window, a signal which was answered a moment later by the window dropping down and a green-covered aldis lamp flashing back a three-second long "blink." Major D'Arcy turned to the sergeant to add: "Make sure every man has a complete kit. Once we are ashore there will be no turning back."

Sergeant Ted Harris saluted, lurched across to a small hatchway and stamped on it. After a lapse of some thirty seconds the hatch was pushed open. Harris hesitated, for down there in the schooner's hold it seemed to him to be darker than the inside of a treacle barrel, but the moment the hatch cover dropped in place a cunningly arranged length of cord whipped up a bucket, revealing a hurricane lamp beneath. Its yellow light flooded the hold, and glistened on the sergeant's dripping oilskins.

Untying the cord about his waist, Harris dropped the

oilskin to the deck, spattering the men with sea water.

"Strike a light, Sarge," one of them protested. "We didn't come here for a flipping shower bath."

"No, you bald-headed Yorkshireman," Harris snapped, though his grin belied the ferocity in his voice. "You came on this trip 'cos you thought it was going to be a picnic, didn't you. Join the army and see the world, eh? I know you, Curly Bates."

"Well, if you don't know me by now you never will," the bald-headed "Curly" Bates grunted, and reaching behind him dipped a mess-tin lid into a bucket and brought it forward, half-filled with steaming coffee. "Here, have a toothful. I won't ask you to have a mouthful . . . there's only about half a gallon left."

"Very funny, very funny indeed," Harris said, but he gratefully gulped off the coffee, saying no more until he had finished it to the last drop. It had been cold work standing on deck. Tossing the mess-tin lid back, he asked: "Now, who the sam-hill brewed coffee? You were warned when you came down here not even to smoke . . . because of the ammunition and explosives we've got . . ."

He was interrupted by an urgent hammering on the hatch cover, and when the lamp was once more shrouded by the bucket Major D'Arcy came down, bringing a shower of salt water with him, for the schooner was now getting closer to the coast and the water was even choppier.

"Thought I had better come down, Sergeant," Major D'Arcy said, opening his oilskin coat and fishing in the right hand pocket of his battledress blouse, "I have just remembered these." In the yellow light he produced a packet of brilliant red, five-pointed cloth stars. These he handed to Sergeant Harris, telling him to issue one to each man.

"We shall be landing on the shores of Yugoslavia in a few minutes," the Major said. "Our task is to contact a group of Partisans and blow up an important railway viaduct. Now that Italy has surrendered the Germans are getting ready to pull out of Yugoslavia. If that railway bridge is blown it means they will have to leave a lot of equipment behind . . . could save a lot of lives, and leave us with a lot of prisoners. Understood?"

Every head nodded soberly.

"The Partisans," the Major continued, "are Yugoslavs who have been fighting the Germans and Italians for a long time, and we have never been able to let them have enough supplies. As a result many of them have had to equip themselves with clothing and arms from their enemies. Which means you will probably find that most of the men we will work with are wearing German or Italian tunics, trousers, greatcoats, boots, and maybe even using German or Italian rifles. So . . . in order that they don't shoot one another they all wear a five-pointed red star . . . such as you have just been given, in their caps. You will do the same. There are a couple of safety pins with each cloth star . . . use them to fasten the star to your cap comforter."

"What happens if any of us get separated from the others?" the questioner was Sam Foster, a fair-haired youngster who looked too mild and youthful to be one of a party of Commandos.

"I am hoping no one will be so unlucky," Major D'Arcy said. "If anyone should . . . try and get to some village. When you meet a villager hold up your clenched fist and shout *Vdekje Fashizmit*. That means Death to Fascism. Anyway, once we are safely ashore, I'll get you all to put it down on paper then you won't forget. All right, Sergeant. I'm going on deck. See that every man's equipment is in order."

"Yessir," and Sergeant Harris gave the Major another parade-ground salute.

When the hatch crashed back in place again, Sergeant Harris checked each man's equipment. In addition to a tommy-gun and six magazines, each carrying twenty rounds of ammunition, there was an automatic pistol, a fighting knife, a clasp knife, two mills grenades, a torch, five days emergency rations, and ten golden sovereigns. The latter were for use if they had to buy from villagers, for paper money was no use.

"Listen you mugs," Sergeant Harris said. "I'll give you one last word of advice. I had a natter with a bloke in Bari who had just come out of Yugoslavia. If you forget what the Major said . . . y'know, that 'death to Fascism stuff,' here's something a bit easier to remember that this Sar'nt Major told me. Stick your clenched fist in the air and say *Zivio Tito* . . . Long Live Tito, and if they cut your throat then it's just too bad."

"Proper educated bloke our sergeant, isn't he?" China Brown chuckled. "*Zivio Tito*. Learned that at Borstal you know. Got his B.A. at Borstal . . . bloomin' awful his B.A. stands for."

There was a chorus of chuckles from the black-faced men standing round. One or two of them had already sensed that there was some kind of an understanding between this Sergeant Harris and three of their comrades. What they did not know was that privates Sam Foster, Curly Bates—the balding Yorkshireman—and China Brown, had been together almost from the beginning of the war. They had been among the first men trained in Commando work, and had earned for themselves the unofficial title of the Fighting Four.

A bang on the hatch cover brought a command to douse the light, and a minute later the thirteen men were scrambling up on to the wet deck. The schooner was now nosing her way inshore at quarter speed, and occasionally grinding her sides in an alarming fashion on unseen rocks.

A heavier than usual bump which caused all the men to drop to one knee to avoid falling, proved fortunate, for within seconds the schooner drove her blunt bows hard on to a beach and came to an abrupt stop which sent the men sliding forward. Had any man been standing erect, he would certainly have taken a serious fall.

A few moments later two of the schooner's crew dropped nimbly over the side and carrying grapnels ashore dug them into the sand, anchoring the vessel. Then Major D'Arcy ordered silence, and everyone looked anxiously ahead, waiting to see a signal light, or hear a voice welcoming them to Yugoslavia.

There was nothing to see and the only sounds came from the waves breaking on the beach, and slapping noisily along the schooner's sides. Major D'Arcy told his men to stand easy, and for almost ten minutes there was an unnatural quiet among the commandos. Major D'Arcy broke the silence.

"Sergeant, take three men and do a recce. These Partisans may be waiting for us to show ourselves. Every man's hand is against them, and they can't afford to take the least chance. There's been a certain amount of treachery going on, and I don't blame these chaps for not walking out into the open. If you make contact, give me a flash on your torch and we'll start unloading."

"And the sooner the better, sir," this from the officer in command of the schooner: "I don't want to be caught round here when daylight comes. Jerry has a number of fast E-boats patrolling the inshore waters, and this tub isn't a fighting ship."

"We won't keep you," the Major assured him. "Now, Sergeant . . . make a sweep of the beach. Don't get more than about a hundred yards or so from us, and if you fail to make contact with anybody within quarter of an hour, come back. That understood."

"Yessir."

Standing at the back of the little crowd of men China Brown whispered to Curly Bates.

"I could save Ted his breath. I know just what he's going to say: 'I want three volunteers . . . er . . . Brown, Bates, Foster. You'll do.' Just see if . . ." and that was as far as China got, for Ted Harris was saying:

"Three volunteers . . . er . . . Foster, Brown, Bates . . . over the side and no noise." He led the way, dropping over the bows and making a splash as he alighted in a foot of water.

"Just like being on holiday, isn't it?" China Brown chuckled as, benefiting by Harris's mistake, he leapt far enough up the beach to avoid wetting his feet. "I never did like paddling."

"Quiet. Extend twenty paces . . . Foster and Brown on my left, Bates on my right. Whistle signals only. You know the code. If I hear a sound from any of you . . . other than whistles, I'll have you all on the peg when we get back."

There were soft chuckles from China Brown and Curly Bates. They knew Ted well enough to realise he did not mean what he said. Each man took a small wooden whistle from his pocket and gripped it between his teeth. Made by a bird watcher in the early days of the war, these whistles could produce the plaintive call of the curlew, the thin piping of a redshank or even the tweet-tweet of a meadow pipit.

Sergeant Harris and his three men had evolved a simple code for night work and obeyed it without hesitation. They had absolute confidence in each other, and moved off into the darkness with little more sound than the soft crunch of rubber boots on the gravel and sand.

The Fighting Four had seen action in the bitterly cold wastes of Norwegian mountains in winter time. They had fought with the Maquis in France, in the African desert and even on the lonely sand dunes of northern Germany. They were tough, and almost without nerves. Yet within five minutes of leaving the water's edge each of them had a growing feeling that he was walking into trouble.

Sergeant Harris was about to give a call on his

whistle which would halt the advance when, from the darkness ahead, came a sound not one of them expected. It was a boyish voice calling:

"Hallo ... Hallo! I am Michaelovitch, and I have got the leader of the Partisans here ... Georgi the Black. Will you show a light? We know you are there but we have no light. The torch is broken."

CHAPTER THREE

TREACHERY

FOR A FEW MOMENTS there was no sound at all, then the short *churring* of a nightjar sounded. Sam Foster moved soundlessly to Ted Harris's side at the signal, while China Brown and Curly Bates moved just as soundlessly uphill. The softest of clicks told of tommy-guns being cocked and safety catches being pushed off. Then Ted broke the silence. The click as he switched on his torch sounded ominously loud; but even if any-one had fired at him they would probably have missed, for the Britisher was lying down and was holding his torch at arm's length.

The brilliant beam of light revealed nothing but rising ground for a moment, then as Ted swung his torch slowly from left to right, it picked up a boy, and by his side stood a tall, heavily moustached man in the rather sloppy traditional dress of Yugoslavia.

"I am coming down," the boy called, shielding his eyes with his hands. "Do not shoot."

Surefooted, even though his hands were up to his eyes, Michaelovitch came down to meet Ted and Sam Foster, and could not conceal his delight when the light thrown back from him revealed the British uniforms.

"Please, we have come for the arms and the food," the youngster said. "I am Michaelovitch Zenel. This man is Georgi the Black. He has the paper which ordered us to come here. We gave the right signal, yes?"

"Why didn't you come down to the beach?" Ted grunted, shifting his torch beam so that it lit up the villainous-looking Georgi the Black. "We have wasted valuable time. Are there only the two of you?"

"No, there are twenty men . . . up the hill, in a cave," Michaelovitch explained. "But, they have been fighting before they got this message, and are almost out of ammunition. So . . . they are afraid to come down until they are sure . . . in case the signal is a trick of the Germans."

"Okay, well tell your friend to bring his men down," Ted ordered, and by this time Curly and China were close, their tommy-guns ready, covering boy and man.

Michaelovitch turned and said something to the man who shrugged and spat back a barrage of Yugoslav, none of which the four Britishers understood. The boy turned to say:

"He asks that you come to the cave to assure his men that all is well. They do not like moving now they are without arms. He says if he shouts they will not come . . . men have been forced to shout before to-day . . . especially if they have a gun pointing at the belly."

"You've got something there," Ted grunted, and turning to face the beach he flashed a quick signal to Major D'Arcy to let him know they were in contact with the Partisans, and that unloading could begin.

"We go now . . . up?" Michaelovitch suggested eagerly.

"What did you say your name was?" Ted asked. "You speak good English."

"My father spent a lot of time in America," was the quick reply. "That is why I speak the English so good. One day I hope to go to America. I am Michaelovitch . . . that is Michael in English."

"Yeah, that's much better," Ted agreed, clapping a friendly hand on the boy's neck. "I think I'll call you Mike."

"That is what my father calls me," and the boy sounded thrilled. "Mike . . . yes, I am happy to be called Mike."

"Like a bit of chocolate?" Sam Foster asked, as they started to walk uphill, the tall Yugoslav leading, his back limned in the beam of Ted Harris's torch.

"Chocolate!" Mike took the bar of nut milk chocolate and, stripping it of its paper wrapping, broke a piece off. He munched silently for a few moments then said: "Please, mister . . . can I put the rest in my pocket. I have a younger brother who has never eaten chocolate like this. Is all British chocolate like this?"

"Some of it's better, kid," China Brown assured him. "Here, take this for your kid brother. I never was much of a one for chocolate." It was a white lie, for China had a sweet tooth, but he was more than rewarded by the gratitude of the fourteen-year-old Mike.

After a gruelling scramble up some two hundred feet of rough hillside they came to a level patch, behind which a rocky wall rose sheer. In the rock there was a cave and though the entrance was shielded by brushwood, they could make out the dim red glow of a small fire.

"Here we have stayed since yesterday morning," Mike announced proudly, dragging some of the brushwood to one side. "I guided Georgi and his men here from the village of Cipili. Come in, please."

Ted stopped at the cave entrance and shone his torch beam into the red-lit interior, and at once there was a half-choked guffaw from China Brown.

"Sorry, Sarge," he hastily apologised, "but you'd think this little lot had just stepped out of that old book . . . y'know, the one where Long John Silver and his parrot were. Strike a light, what a bunch they are. Fred Karno's circus and no mistake."

The light did show up the Yugoslav's badly. They were a wolfish-looking crowd, badly dressed, dirty, unshaved, and every man carrying at least one automatic at his waist.

Yet as Ted and his three men walked in the crowd rose from their places by the fire, and bowed politely while Giuseppe, the Italian deserter, cried out:

"They *are* British. Ah, my friends. It ees good to see real men again," and he came forward with both hands out-thrust.

Ted eyed him coldly, gave him a nod, and then turned to look for Mike. To him he said:

"Let's not waste time, son, we've got to get the stores unloaded as soon as possible, and the boat has to get well out to sea before dawn."

"Yes," Mike agreed nervously, "but Georgi insists that he introduces you to his men. They are all anxious to shake hands with British soldiers."

"Okay, but let's get cracking." Ted knew that Major D'Arcy's temper would not be very sweet if his "recce" patrol kept away too long. He had stipulated no more than ten minutes, and that time limit had been about reached already.

The four Britishers lined up and, through Mike, Georgi began to introduce his men. The first four were shaking hands when Georgi turned and crashed his fist at Ted's jaw. It was a treacherous blow. Ted reeled into China Brown, and as he did so the rest of the men piled in.

It was a cunningly contrived trick, for in order to shake hands the four Britishers had shouldered their tommy-guns, and each of them was already gripping the hand of a Yugoslav.

They never had a real chance of fighting off the attack. Not that they went down without doing some damage. One of the Yugoslavs took a left hook in the solar plexus and sat on the fire. Blazing sticks were scattered all about and the screeches of agony bore testimony to the heat of the little fire.

For perhaps three minutes the only sounds were grunts and gasps, the smack of a fist on a face; snarls of pain; the thump as a man reeled backwards and hitting the rocky wall of the cave slumped down, every ounce of fight knocked out of him.

Sheer weight of numbers told. One after the other the Fighting Four went down under a tangle of bodies. One after the other they were overpowered, and pinned face down. Then, with a gun muzzle boring into the back of the neck, they were forced to kneel while their webbing was jerked off them, their arms taken away and their wrists securely tied.

Mike had stared in absolute amazement at this unexpected treachery. Then, as he realised there was nothing he could do, he hurried to the open air and vanished. When the embers of the fire were scraped together again the four Britishers were lined up, sitting against the side wall. They were completely and utterly helpless. Each had his wrists tied behind his back, and a length of cord went from his wrists to his ankles, so that he could not even lie with his legs stretched out straight.

In helpless fury they watched Georgi the Black examining the tommy-guns, and it was pretty obvious that he was no fool with them. After checking each weapon in turn he handed them out, then led the way out of the cave. Two of the crowd were left behind to guard the prisoners, and one of these, the Italian, promptly came over to search them.

"Ah, Eenglish cigarettes, mucha better than Balkan cigarillos," he enthused, as he gathered four lots of cigarettes. He lit one, handed a packet to the other guard, then said: "Once I am hotel waiter in London, so I spikka da English good, eh. You do not expect to have treatment such as thees, eh. No!" and he laughed uproariously.

"So you are an Italian, are you?" Ted asked, and somehow curbed a desire to say what he thought about Italian soldiers. He had to try and get this man on their side, and do it quickly. "Do you not know that Italy has surrendered. Mussolini has been thrown out, and your country is now fighting against the Germans. We are not supposed to be enemies now, but allies. If you undid these ropes we . . ."

"Ah, no-no-no-no!" the Italian said, laughing and

spreading his hands in a gesture of disapproval. "I leave da Italian army long ago. No fight for Mussolini. Now I fight for *Ustachi*. You hear of them. No! I tell you. *Ustachi* are Yugoslav men who side with Germans. Good until this past month or so . . . now we think Germans lose war. So we fight for ourselves. We take things from churches . . . gold candlesticks, chalices . . . very valuable. Very soon we divide the loot and . . . poof! . . . we vanish."

"So you are not Partisans?"

"No, no. Never. This man you theenk is Georgi the Black is actually Dravadavitch. Everyone is afraid of Dravadavitch. But I am not. We make plenty of money . . . then go, as I say, *poof* . . . we vanish, and it ees good. Yes."

"Be good when you feel a rope round your neck," Ted snapped. "Look, I'm giving you a chance. Set us free, and I'll take you in as a deserter from the Italian army. When you get ashore at Bari nobody is going to ask any questions about you. You will be free."

"You listen to me, Mr. Three-stripe-sergeant—you see I know something about the Briteesh army. Very soon you will hear guns popping. Dravadavitch is clever man. He go down to shore . . . maybe he speak to your men, more likely he just shoot them down. After . . ." and the Italian paused long enough to pop half a block of Ted's chocolate ration into his mouth, then went on: "Afterwards . . . he and the others breeng all things from the ship up here. Maybe he seenk ship; maybe not. Maybe we go away in ship. Dravadavitch will decide. He is clever man."

"I hope you'll remember I gave you a chance—when

you are a prisoner," Ted snapped. "As for Dravadavitch catching our men napping . . . what a hope. You wait and see."

Ted sounded confident, but he was waiting and listening with an anxious and a heavy heart. He had flashed a signal to Major D'Arcy that all was well and that the unloading of stores from the schooner could begin. He knew how anxious everyone was to get the schooner away, because of the risk of her being caught by an E-boat when dawn came. Because of this every man jack would be busy . . . hauling stores up from the hold and stacking them on the beach. The Major would not set a guard. It would seem a waste of a valuable labourer, since Ted had given him the "Okay."

Five minutes of silence, with the Italian finishing the chocolate and smoking in between each mouthful, then came the sound Ted was afraid of. A sudden, distant rattle of automatic fire. Ted and his pals recognised it as British tommy-gun fire, but it did not console them. Dravadavitch and his men had seized the tommy-guns belonging to the three commandos, and would be using them with all the advantages which come from a surprise attack.

Ted squirmed like an eel, trying to loosen his wrist bonds. He could imagine what was happening on the beach. The crew would have rigged up a derrick and a dim deck light to give them some illumination to work by. There would be men on the beach, taking the stores from those on deck and stacking them above high-water-mark. Not one of them would have a weapon handy.

If Dravadavitch knew anything at all about fighting,

he would get close in and the battle would be over in a few minutes. Several bursts from close range would finish off the men on deck and those on the beach. Then if he rushed the schooner, he could pen the others up in the ship's hold.

Ted closed his eyes and groaned. If he had been in Dravadavitch's place he knew how easy it would have been. The worst part of it all was the fact that Major D'Arcy had sent Ted and his three men out on to the beach to make sure it was safe to begin unloading.

"They say there's a sucker born every minute," he groaned. "Listen to that tommy-gun fire! Cor, how we walked into it, eh? Strike a light, I never thought I'd be taken in by a kid. I don't suppose I'd have trusted that bloke Georgi . . ."

"Not Georgi, *Dravadavitch*," the Italian called out, enjoying Ted's distress. "He is great fighter. Very great fighter."

"You don't expect an innocent-looking kid to be a traitor, do you?" Ted went on, ignoring the Italian. "Did I buy it. If my hands were free I'd rip my stripes off I'm that disgusted with myself."

"If you were a sucker, what about me?" Sam asked, hoping to console Ted. "I gave him half my chocolate ration."

"What do you reckon they'll do with us?" China Brown asked, trying to turn the conversation. "I know we're in correct army uniform, and should be treated as prisoners of war; but with stinkers like these you never know . . . ouch!"

"You call me stinker?" it was the Italian who had put his foot in China's ribs. "You say anytheeng like so bad again I put my foot in your teeth. And listen . . . I answer your question. What weel be done with you, you ask. I tell you. To-morrow . . . tat-ta-tat-tat . . . and it ees fineesh. I know Dravadavitch. He never keeps prisoner."

After that there was silence until the first of the Yugoslavs returned from the beach staggering under a sack of tinned foodstuffs. He was followed by others, and for the next two hours Dravadavitch and his men worked hard. There were some three tons of supplies aboard the schooner, and the loot had to be carried up some two hundred feet to the cave, no light task.

The Italian started cooking a meal when the first sack of food was dumped at his feet, and by the time the last man had dropped the last load the cave carried an appetising odour. Whatever the Italian deserter was, he could cook, if the smell was anything to go by.

Dravadavitch went to have a last look across the dark hillside, and this brought him close to the four Britishers. By his start of surprise it was obvious he had forgotten all about them. Now, a snarl on his face, he shouted to some of the men crowding round the fire, and at his order Ted, Sam, Curly and China were jerked to their feet. For a moment they wondered if they were going to be set free, for the rope connecting their wrists to their ankles was cut, but it was only so that they could stand upright. A minute later they were standing with their backs to the end wall of the cave while Dravadavitch himself checked that the tommy-gun he had picked up was loaded and cocked.

"Do you wish to be blindfolded?" the Italian asked,

wiping his greasy hands. "Our leader weel do the thing correct."

For a moment Ted Harris was tempted to ask for a bandage across his eyes, just in case it gave him a chance when the Italian came up to do it; but he decided it was only wasting time. He could never hope to get away. Between him and the cave entrance were all Dravadavitch's men. A tommy-gun might blast a way through . . . an unarmed man, especially one with his wrists tied behind his back, would not stand a chance.

"Shoot and be hanged to you," Ted snarled, and taking a quick sideways glance at his three companions said: "Sorry it had to end like this, chaps. So long Sam, Curly, China . . . see you again, on the other side."

"So long, Sergeant Harris," Sam Foster said. "And thanks for all you've done for me. I owe you a lot."

Ted gulped. Poor Sam. He was always the one to have his leg pulled, yet he was as good a soldier as ever donned uniform. He stood there now, erect, his flaxen hair shining in the firelight, his face still smeared with the boot-black camouflage they had wiped on before going aboard the old schooner back in the Italian port of Bari.

Silence fell over the cave. One or two of the Yugoslavs stuck their fingers into their ears, for the staccato crash of a tommy-gun would be like thunder in the confines of the cave.

"Hope he fires a long burst, Ted," China Brown spoke out of the corner of his mouth. "If he does somebody else will get hurt. There'll be ricocheting bullets flying everywhere."

"Ready?" It was the Italian again.

"Get cracking," Ted said coldly, and stared at Dravadavitch. He watched the Yugoslav settle the tommy-gun butt firmly against his hip, and closed his eyes for a split second, wondering if he would hear the crash of the shots.

Bang!

CHAPTER FOUR

A LION IN LAMB'S CLOTHING

TED INSTINCTIVELY opened his eyes, and was in time to see a ruddy glow outside the cave entrance. It lit up the pile of brushwood for a second, throwing shafts of red light on the Yugoslavs who were all turning, and cowering. They had used too many hand grenades not to know the distinctive crack which these explosives make.

There was a crackling as shrapnel slashed and cut through the branches of brushwood. One man gave a howl of pain as a sliver of hot metal took the top off his right hand little finger.

A moment later the red glow was gone and everyone was blinking in the subdued light of the fire. For perhaps five seconds Dravadavitch and his men stood as if petrified, then they moved. Like startled cats they scattered, jumping to one side or the other of the cave. Most of them had piled their tommy-guns only a few minutes earlier, but practically every man had a pistol of some kind, and these were produced and cocked ready for action.

"Put out the fire," Dravadavitch whispered, but as one of his men made a grab for a pan of stewing bully beef and tinned vegetables, a voice from the outside halted him.

"I give you five seconds to lay down your guns."

"Stone the crows, Mike!" Curly Bates muttered. "It's the kid!"

The Yugoslav who had been about to extinguish the fire drew back against the cave wall.

"For pete's sake do something, son," Ted Harris whispered anxiously. "If you don't you've lost your chance. They'll get over the shock, then it'll be too late."

Dravadavitch's men *were* getting over the shock. Word was being passed round. One man to throw his coat over the fire, the other to dash for the cave entrance, firing as they went. Some might die, but others would get out into the open. In the cave they were worse than rats in a trap. A sustained burst from a tommy-gun would kill or wound every man jack.

"Five . . ." Michaelovitch called from the darkness outside, and a moment later something crashed through the thin screen of brushwood and rolled along the cave floor towards the fire. It was a hand grenade!

"Down!" Ted Harris snapped and slumped to the ground, being beaten to it by Curly Bates. China Brown and Sam Foster were only a second behind their comrades. In a confined space like this the destructive effects of a hand grenade would be fantastic. Segmented metal would fly everywhere, ricocheting off the floor, walls and ceiling of the cave, and inflicting the most dreadful wounds.

Dravadavitch and his men realised this too. Panic-stricken screams mingled with curses as men rose from crouching positions along the walls and fairly hurled themselves towards the back of the cave. It was every man for himself, and every man's ambition was to get on the floor, and have one or more of his companions between him and the grenade.

Ted Harris found himself counting aloud: "One . . . two . . . three . . . four . . . five . . . six . . . seven." The average fuse in a grenade was seven seconds, and when he mouthed the word seven he closed his eyes again and tried to curl himself into an even tighter ball. Everyone else was doing the same thing.

It was while they were doing this that a slim youngster dived through a gap in the brushwood at the cave entrance and darting towards the fire grabbed the grenade. Seven seconds had passed and there had been no explosion. In those seven seconds Michaelovitch had come in and was now standing by the fire, the grenade in his hand.

"I had not taken out the pin," he yelled, and while men lifted their heads to see what was happening the youngster hooked his left thumb into the split ring of the grenade's safety pin, and with a flourish he whipped the pin out. This time the grenade was really *live*. If he dropped it, there would be no second chance for anyone.

For perhaps ten seconds there was a stupefied silence. Ted Harris began to struggle to a sitting position, and the movement brought a threat.

"Move, and I throw the grenade!" The threat was spoken in the Yugoslav tongue for in the flickering light of the fire it was impossible for the youngster to see who was moving in the huddled figures.

"Mike . . . Mike . . . it's me, the British sergeant," Ted spluttered. "Let me get to my feet."

"One only," came the warning. "If anyone else moves . . . I throw this. See . . . the pin is out," and he swung his left hand so that the safety pin whirled on its split ring round and round his thumb, flickering a little in the firelight.

Michaelovitch came nearer, so near that Ted Harris wanted to warn him to stay where he was. As if guessing his thoughts the boy said harshly:

"I am not afraid, Britisher. If any man shoots me . . . the grenade falls and then it will explode. I may die . . . but if I do, there will be many others." Then in Yugoslav he said the same thing.

There was a breathless silence among the huddle of men. There were at least half a dozen who held pistols, and any one of them could have quietly lifted his hand, taken aim, and killed the youngster where he stood; yet not a man moved. They were all thinking the same thing: if the grenade goes off I may be killed.

Sergeant Harris got to his feet. Carefully he strode over the men on the ground.

"Got a knife, Mike?" Ted asked. He was trying hard to sound composed, but his heart was thumping madly. It seemed no more than a few seconds since he had been standing with his back to the wall, facing what seemed certain execution by the tommy-gun of Dravadavitch. Now there was a slim chance they might get away.

Still keeping his eyes on the tense figures before him, Michaelovitch felt for his knife. Ted turned so that he had his back to the boy, yet did not obstruct his view. He winced several times as the knife slashed skin as well as rope. Then his hands were free.

"You'll have to hold them there for a minute or

two," he muttered when, with the blood surging back into his fingers he was attacked by the biting agony of "pins and needles."

Five minutes ticked by; five minutes which must have seemed like five hours to the Yugoslavs lying on the ground, and as long to the three Britishers still tied-up at the back of the cave. Then, with feeling creeping back into his fingers, Ted walked across to the stacked tommy-guns. Blood was running down his right hand where the knife which cut him free had also cut the palm of his hand. It was stinging, but he hardly felt it. From despair he had risen in minutes to triumph. From being a trussed-up captive he now had a score of prisoners, but they were almost all in possession of arms of some kind.

There were some anxious minutes until Sam, China and Curly had been freed and had got back the use of their hands. Ted remained calm and watchful, the tommy-gun held in the crook of his right hand, but his fingers never left the trigger. One false move on the part of any of the Yugoslavs would have brought a withering blast of fire.

"Right," Ted murmured when Sam, the last to be freed, was flexing his fingers and agreeing that the agonising "pins and needles" of returning circulation were growing less. "Now, disarm these beauties. Then we'll have their boots off. Throw them down the hill-side. If I remember right, the stones of that slope would cut a mule's feet to ribbons. If our prisoners are barefooted, they'll think twice about trying to run away."

When all the arms had been collected and twenty

pairs of boots had been tossed down the hill, Ted sent Sam and China down to the beach to see if the schooner was still there, and if there were any wounded men needing attention. He ordered the Italian who had gloated over them, and threatened they would be dead before morning, to get busy and cook some fresh food.

The stew, which had already been overcooked, was about to be thrown away when the young Yugoslav, Mike, raised his hands in horrified protest.

"Not to throw it away, sir," he pleaded. "Back in the hills there are over a hundred children, and some mothers, who are starving."

Ted frowned. He had not yet made up his mind about Mike. The youngster had saved them from death, that was certain, but so far as Ted was concerned, he was also the one who had led them into the trap.

"There's plenty of grub here," he said after a moment's thought. "Give that to our prisoners. We weren't supposed to be feeding children, but maybe there'll be enough left over to give them some."

When Sam and China got back they reported the beach clear except for two grapnels and some empty cartridge cases. Questioned through Mike, Dravada-vitch sulkily agreed that he had been afraid to go in close, and had contented himself with firing at the schooner from a distance. It had given the Major a chance to cut his hawsers and get out to sea—though he had been forced to leave his supplies on the beach.

"When can we radio?" Ted asked, cheering up wonderfully. "Bari gave us a time."

"Ten o'clock to-morrow morning, Sarge," Sam
Foster agreed. "They won't be listening in on our
special wave-length until then."

"Okay. Then we'll get some shut-eye. We need some
sleep. China, you'll take the first two hours. Curly
will take over from you, Sam from Curly."

"Hm, now let me see, who'll take over after that?"
Curly Bates jeered. "Or will it be broad daylight?
Strike a light, Sarge. You're the kindest man I ever
knew. Always thinking about your men, aren't you
. . . You ain't going to do a watch."

"When you get three stripes on your arm, my lad,"
Ted grunted, winking, "you'll know that you are
supposed to *command* men, not coddle 'em. And whoever is on guard when reveille goes, remember to bring
me a mug of steaming char . . . strong and with lots
of sugar in it. Good night . . . oh, and if these Yugoslavs start making any noise . . . shoot the lot. Did you
hear that, you Eyetie deserter. I said . . . shoot the lot.
Just tell your pals that if they disturb my sleep . . .
it'll be the last thing they ever do."

He was chuckling softly as he lay down, for the
Italian deserter was already passing on what he had
said to the others. When China wakened Curly Bates,
Ted Harris lifted his head. One moment he seemed to
be sound asleep, the next he was wide-awake. Throughout the rest of the night he lay with eyes closed, but his
hand never left the trigger guard of his tommy-gun.

It was over breakfast that he spoke to Michaelovitch.
The youngster had been very quiet ever since waking
and Ted stuck a finger under the boy's chin, making
him look up.

"What's the matter, son? Are you wondering why I haven't thanked you for saving our lives last night?"

Michaelovitch shook his head.

"I came back for two reasons," he said doggedly. "One because I did not want the man Sam to die. He had been so kind. He gave me chocolate, even without me asking for food."

"And the other reason," Ted asked, as Michaelovitch hesitated.

"I came back for food," and like a flood he poured out his story of the children and women who were starving in the hills. He had been their best provider. He had gone time after time to the farms around and stolen from the fields. He had gone to Cavtat, a seaside resort a few miles to the north, and there had stolen from the German garrison supplies. "We never have enough. Now there is plenty of food here, and I thought you might give me some for my friends."

Ted sat staring into space for a few moments. He had been suspicious of the boy, blaming him for the way he had led them up to the cave where Dravada-vitch's men had ambushed them.

"We could do something for them, Sarge," China Brown suggested. "After all, we've got lashings of grub, haven't we?"

"It all depends on what headquarters in Bari decide," Ted finally muttered. "If they sent another schooner to-night, with more men, then we'd have to go on with the job. Don't forget, we came here for something more than landing supplies."

"Then you cannot help us," the boy asked gravely.

"Look, Mike, I owe you my life—and that was pretty important to me. These," and he was grinning as he indicated China Brown and Curly Bates, "they don't matter very much. Two a penny, if you know what I mean. But as far as I'm concerned there's only one Sergeant Harris—so I'm grateful. You are going to get all the grub you need. A lot of this was for the Partisans. Okay, there are no Partisans here, so you get it. How's that?"

To his dismay Mike burst into tears.

"That's just like you," China Brown said, stepping forward and folding the boy's thin body in his arms. "If you ever have a family of your own I can see 'em all marching around like rookies on a parade ground. Now, Mike, don't cry. What he said he means. We'll see your pals have plenty of grub."

Gradually Mike's sobs died away and then he dried his eyes on the back of his grubby right hand.

"I am sorry for crying," he gulped. "It is so long since anyone was kind."

"Yeah, we know," China said soothingly. "You just go an' watch Sam Foster wiggle his morse key. He's trying to speak to our top brass in Italy."

"Top brass?" Mike queried. "What does that mean?"

"The people in headquarters," Ted Harris hurriedly explained. "We have to report to them about this time how we are getting on. We'll have to tell them that only we four are ashore, and that we don't know what happened to the schooner."

While Sam was alternately hammering out morse then listening for a reply, Ted and China Brown checked the stores—guns, ammunition, grenades, explosives and food. There was almost a ton of food, mostly in tins, though there was a sack or two of flour.

Their prisoners sat disconsolately watching, guarded by Curly Bates, who, with a tommy-gun under his right arm and a grenade in his left hand, strolled backwards and forwards, whistling a variety of tunes, and looking as happy as a sandboy.

Finally Sam Foster made contact with Bari. For an hour, then, Ted Harris was busy decoding the signals which Sam picked up. China, watching, finally broke the silence with an exasperated:

"What the heck's the matter, Ted? You look as if you've just had fourteen days home leave cancelled. Bad news?"

"Oh, no," Ted waxed sarcastic. "I always look like this when I've had *good* news. Why don't you be your age, China? It's bad news. We've got to hide the arms, explosives and grub. They're going to send another bunch as soon as possible to do the railway viaduct. In the meantime we hide and wait for about four days."

"Well, what's wrong with that?" China was frowning.

"Will you please get out of reach," Ted pleaded, "or I'll forget myself and crown you with a hunk of rock. The orders are to hide *all* the food and stores, and ourselves until a fresh bunch land here. We can't do it."

China was going to ask why, but Sam Foster stopped him.

"The kids in the hills," he explained. "Mike's pals.

Ted promised to feed them, and that means taking the grub."

"That's it in a nutshell," Ted added grimly. "If we obey orders, the kids starve. If we feed the kids and another bunch of our lads come ashore they'll have no supplies. Now, China, see if you can laugh that off. You are a smart guy. What would you do?"

CHAPTER FIVE

CHINA BROWN'S PLAN

FOR A MOMENT or so China stood silent, then the corners of his mouth began to turn up, and soon he was grinning.

"I'm surprised at you, Sarge, asking a mere private for advice. 'Course, me being the sort of bloke I am I'll . . ."

"Cut the cackle and get to the hosses," Ted snapped. "This isn't the time for being funny. If you have an idea . . . we'll have it. It's probably crazy, anyway."

"Not crazy, Sarge, just simple," China protested. "What's to stop us feeding the kids, blowing the viaduct, then radioing Bari to tell them they needn't send any more troops as we've done the trick. They can just send a liner to take us back in the comfort and luxury we deserve."

Sam Foster looked at China, then shot a quick glance towards Ted to see how he took the idea. Young Mike's face had brightened at China's "plan." To him it seemed everything he could wish for.

"It's simple," Ted agreed. "But according to Mike, here, the children who need the grub are about ten miles inland . . . up some mountain. There are four of us, and I'm no mule."

53

"What about this bunch of thugs?" the question came from Curly who had been listening intently. "There's a score of *carriers* here, don't forget."

Ted Harris pondered for a moment, then he motioned Mike to stand aside. He called Curly to join him, and said quietly:

"Listen, you mugs. I don't want to break my word to this youngster. But for him we'd be dead."

"You needn't tell us that, Sarge, we know," China Brown agreed.

"I've just had orders from Bari to hide the grub and stores and to keep under cover until a new bunch of fellows can be got over. If we take this grub into the hills for these starving kids . . . it means we've got to prevent Headquarters sending more chaps here. If they think there's grub here they won't send a second batch."

"Couldn't we do this demolition job, as China suggested, then radio Bari?" Sam suggested. "That would solve the problem."

"That's what I'm coming to," Ted said tersely. "If you are game I'm willing to chance my arm. If it doesn't come off . . . it could mean the death of some of our blokes, and it'll certainly mean me being stripped of my stripes."

"That'd be terrible," China said grinning, but wiped the grin off his face immediately at a scowl from Harris. "No, I didn't mean that, Sarge. I think we can do it."

"We've *got* to do it," Ted snapped. "Now, pin your ears back and listen. I know what we have to do, you don't. You've got to get the details firmly fixed in your thick heads, and that viaduct has to be blown if there's only one of us left. Okay?"

"Okay." Sam, China and Curly echoed the word, then listened intently as Ted went into details of where the all-important railway viaduct was, and where demolition charges would have to be laid to do the greatest damage. He made each of them repeat the details in turn.

In the next two hours they made up twenty bundles of food, each weighing about 50 pounds. It made up almost half a ton of supplies, and ought to feed even a starving crowd of a hundred for several days. Ted Harris had decided that he and his three friends would carry two spare tommy-guns each, and as much ammunition as possible, two or three grenades, and the explosive charges for the demolition work.

"Did you say you weren't a mule, Sarge?" China Brown asked when he tested the weight he was going to carry. "You were dead right, too. This isn't a pack for a mule. It's a pack for a flippin' elephant."

"You'll carry it," Ted growled. "If you want to change and carry mine, I don't mind."

China tested Ted's pack, and shook his head. Ted Harris never asked his friends to do more than he was doing, and his pack was the heaviest of the lot.

They had a big meal, at the same time feeding their hungry prisoners. Ted warned the Yugoslavs that they would be fastened together with a line round each man's neck, connecting him to the man in front of him and the man behind. If there was any attempt to break away, there would be shooting, quick and accurate.

"You can tell 'em," Ted ordered Mike, "that we're

taking no chances. We know that if one of them gets away it'll be the finish of us. So . . . we don't mean any to leave the bunch."

An hour before dusk Giuseppe called to Ted and pointed out that they could not possibly carry loads across the mountain tracks unless they had their footwear. Ted swore softly. He had forgotten that the night before he had ordered the Yugoslavs to doff their boots, and had watched them thrown over the lip of the hill. He ordered Sam to release the Italian.

"And listen, pal," Ted said grimly. "You find every one of those boots. If you don't . . . you'll be the last to have something for your feet. Understand."

"Si . . . si, Sergeant," Giuseppe babbled. "I find, and I do not run away. I do not like theese German pigs at all. Better be prisoner of Briteesh than of Germans."

"Don't try to suck up to me," Ted growled disgustedly, "or I'll give you a clip across the earhole. Go on, get weaving."

For twenty minutes Giuseppe combed the hillside, he found a good many of the boots easily enough, but there were still three missing as the light began to fade. Sam Foster went down to help him, while Curly Bates watched from above, his gun cocked, ready. Two more boots were found, and now there was only one missing . . . it was Giuseppe's right boot.

"All right," Ted bawled down. "Come on . . . you'll have to wrap your foot in rags. We can't waste any more time."

The Italian nodded dejectedly, took a pace or two up the hill, then paused to have a last look round. Ted yelled to him to come up and Giuseppe waved a hand to show he had heard, then gave a yelp of triumph.

"I see it, Sergeant. I see it," and he pointed. "You letta me fetch it?"

"Be quick."

Scrambling a dozen yards across the hill Giuseppe reached down, picked up a boot, waved it in triumph, then bent to drag it on. Sam was already up beside Ted. The prisoners were busy lacing their boots. Everything was ready for a start, and it was then that the Italian made his break for liberty.

He started to climb up the hill, then suddenly turned and running like a frightened hare, reached the shelter of a rock just as Ted Harris fired a short burst over his head.

"Get down to him, Sam," Ted ordered, "and if he won't come back . . . shoot him. The lives of all of us are in his hands if he gets away."

Sam started down the hill, taking giant strides which ate up the distance in seconds. He had taken many a bruising tumble when he had been introduced to mountains in far-away Scotland, but he had learned his lessons well, and was now as sure-footed as a mountain goat.

Giuseppe also had experience on mountains, having been conscripted into one of the crack Alpine regiments, the famous Bersaglieri, famed for their exploits in hill fighting. What was more, fear gave wings to his feet, and the farther down the hill he got the more cover there was.

Rocks and scrubby bushes gave him cover. Twice he screamed and dropped out of sight when Sam fired a short burst, but each time unharmed, he ran rabbit fashion, crouching low so that Sam could see nothing of him. When the young Britisher finally got down to the beach he had to admit that Giuseppe had made his getaway.

He had chosen the moment well, for the light was fading quickly now, and short of cordoning off the area, the Italian could not be caught. Sam went back to the cave, glum-faced and apologetic.

"Sorry, Sarge."

"We can't always win," Ted snapped. "I wish it had been one of the Yugoslavs, though, instead of him."

"Why?" this from Curly Bates.

"I've got to tell you everything, haven't I?" Ted murmured, shaking his head. "If it had been a Yugoslav he might not have dared to go to Jerry headquarters to tell them about us. As it is, the Italians have been fighting with the Germans for four years. He'll likely go to the nearest German outpost, report that a party of British have landed, and maybe indicate where we are heading."

"He doesn't know," China pointed out.

"Don't be silly," Ted replied. "He knows we've packed the food. He knows we are not going to try and swim the Adriatic. There's only one way we can go . . . inland. Anyway, no use crying over spilt milk. Get those blokes on their feet. Mike . . . are you ready? You lead the way, and march quick. Can we get to this place where the children are before morning? "

"I think maybe yes," Mike agreed. "Can I have a gun?"

Ted hesitated for a moment then shook his head.

"No, better for you not to be armed," he said. "If we are caught we are entitled to be treated as ordinary prisoners of war. We are in British army uniform. If you are caught carrying arms . . . it's different. I think they'd probably shoot you. The Germans are getting nervous. They're afraid of the people rising. So . . . no gun. Sorry," and he clapped a friendly hand on Mike's shoulders.

A few minutes later the trek inland began. It was tough going, and slow. Mike knew the country inland, but not near the shore, so they had to walk without the benefit of tracks. Nor could they go near the village of Cipili, where there was a road. German patrols visited the village, and sometimes stayed the night. Ted dare not risk a clash at this stage.

Progress was not so slow for the Italian, Giuseppe. He waited in the cover of a clump of bushes, torn for several minutes between triumph and terror until he saw Sam Foster go back up the hill. When darkness finally shrouded the country the Italian made his way back to the cave. It was a bold move, for if the Britishers were still there they would not give him another chance of freedom. Yet he had to get to the cave to procure some evidence to show the Germans. If he could persuade them that a party of British commandos had landed, then they would probably treat him well. If they thought he was just another Italian deserter who was crawling back to them because he was hungry, they might easily clap him against a wall and shoot him.

Giuseppe entered the cave about an hour after Ted and the rest had left. He rummaged among the equipment there, and finally took a spare radio set. It was cunningly made to fit into a case no bigger than a large brief case, and Giuseppe knew the Germans would accept this as bona-fide evidence, for the batteries were date stamped.

The distance from the cave to the little seaside resort of Cavtat was only about five miles, but it was three o'clock in the morning before Giuseppe made his way to the German headquarters, and with the wireless set on his back, marched up to the sleepy sentry and gave himself up.

His persistent demands to be taken to the officer wore down the guard corporal and at half past three, while the Italian drank a mug of ersatz coffee and ate some bread, the news that a party of British commandos had landed and were heading inland was being given by telephone to German headquarters at Dubrovnik, the one-time fashionable Yugoslav seaside resort.

At four o'clock Giuseppe was marching south again with a strong party of Germans to reveal the cave and the stores. At five o'clock by means of a portable radio they had brought along with them, the patrol confirmed that Giuseppe's story was true. There were stores in a cave. They looked as if they had been brought quite recently, and there were, in fact, the still warm ashes of a fire in the cave.

At dawn a Fieseler Storch light aircraft took off from a small airfield a few miles from Dubrovnik, to scour the hills behind where Giuseppe said the Britishers had landed. While it was flying through the grey of early morning, lorry loads of German troops were getting under way. They rumbled along the lonely roads, converging on the area where the Italian thought the commandos would be.

At six o'clock, as the sun was tipping the hilltops gold, headquarters at Dubrovnik received a message from the Storch spotter plane. The pilot had seen a party of between 20 and 30 men marching in single file up a mountain slope. They had scattered into nearby bushes when he flew over, and if he had not been lucky in catching a glimpse of them the moment he skimmed over the top of the mountain, they would have passed unnoticed.

"Try to keep them in sight," was the command from German headquarters at Dubrovnik. "We are sending troops to the area at once, and will despatch a Stuka dive bomber to keep them busy."

CHAPTER SIX

ATTACK FROM THE AIR

BECAUSE of the mountains no one heard the sound of the Fieseler Storch plane until seconds after it came flying perilously close to the side of the hill along which the party was making its weary way. It was instinctive for China, Sam and Curly to raise their tommy-guns, but Ted Harris halted them before a single trigger could be squeezed:

"Down, everybody," he yelled: "Down . . . down . . . down!"

If the Yugoslav prisoners did not understand the word "down," they knew what was likely to happen when a German plane came upon a file of men who were not German soldiers. Strafing from the air was unpleasant, and they all dived for cover.

The Fieseler Storch flew away, but droned back several minutes later when Ted had got his line on the march one more. Again everyone dived for cover, and again the spotter plane flew away.

"Mike, how far are we off the cave?" Ted asked, hurrying to the front where the youngster was leading the way after the second interruption.

"Another 50 metres up."

"Fifty metres . . . hm . . . a hundred and fifty feet. All right, we'll see if we can make it before the plane comes round for the third time."

They were no more than fifty feet from the large cave when the Fieseler Storch came round for the third time, and this time the pilot made the mistake of flying too low in an effort to identify the people on the hillside.

For the third time everybody scattered, but Ted Harris had already made up his mind that the German pilot was too interested in them, and had to be dealt with. He had passed the word to his three men, and after diving into the bushes Ted rolled swiftly on to his back and fired a long burst into the belly of the plane. Even as his gun began its staccato chattering two other tommy-guns joined in, then a third.

The Fieseler Storch is a small plane, with a relatively low speed. It is ideal for target spotting, and for going to places where landing grounds are extremely small. But it is not suited for ground strafing, or low flying over enemy troops. It flies too slow.

Four accurately-placed bursts of tommy-gun fire from a range of little more than a hundred feet was more than the plane could stand. It was a tribute to the accuracy of the fire that not only did the engine stop, but the plane keeled over at once, suggesting that the pilot had died at his controls.

There was something rather startling in the silence which followed. A moment before there had been the savage tat-tat-tat-tat-tat of four guns chattering viciously, and above that sound the thunder of the engine. Now there was no sound at all save a faint whistle as the Fieseler Storch dived down.

A few moments later the tiny plane struck the wooded hillside some two hundred feet lower down.

It bounced into the air, cartwheeled twice, then burst into flame as it collapsed on its broken back. Ted Harris lifted his hand gravely to a salute, an action which made Mike stare in amazement.

"What did you do that for, Sergeant?" he asked. "You saluted."

"I saluted a brave man," Ted's voice was quiet. There was no triumph in it.

"But he was a German," Mike protested.

"He was doing what he had been told to do," Ted replied. "I didn't want to shoot him. He saw us and it was his duty, no doubt, to make sure who we were and then report to his officers. He risked his life to obey orders. He's dead now, but he was a brave man just the same."

Mike scratched at his mop of hair. There were some things about Britishers which puzzled him, and this was one of them. Then Ted took his thoughts to other things.

"Come on, Mike, things might get very tough soon. I'll bet that pilot has radioed his headquarters that we are here. No doubt he thinks we are a gang of Partisans . . . which probably means the Germans will be out after us. What happens when they catch Partisans?"

Mike stared at him for a moment, his eyes round and solemn. Then he lifted his hands as if he was holding a rifle.

"Bang . . . bang!" he said, then turned and began to walk up the hillside again. There was no doubt what he meant. Partisans were executed by firing squad if they fell into German hands. Although this had been well known to Ted before, his admiration for the men and women who were hitting back at the enemy from the hills increased.

Five minutes later he followed Mike into a large cave. At first glance it appeared to be empty. Then Mike gave a peculiar whistle, and at once a vague dark mass at the far end of the cave broke up into a mass of boys and girls, and a few women.

Their look-out had both heard and seen the Fieseler Storch flying about, and then he had heard the chatter of tommy-guns. He had not seen the light aeroplane shot down, but he had heard the clatter of approaching feet as the file of men moved along a scree. The boy had rushed into the cave, and the six women had ushered the children into the darkest part of their refuge. They all squatted as close to one another as possible, their faces turned away from the light streaming into the cave entrance. Anyone just looking into the darkness might well have thought it held no life.

Young Mike was almost overwhelmed by a mass of children, all of them wanting to know if he had brought back any food. The sight of the pinched faces of the children brought a lump to the throat of Sam Foster, and even the tough, wise-cracking Curly was so shaken that he looked along the line of bundles which the weary Yugoslavs had dropped, and began opening one of them which he knew contained pound tins of bully beef.

Ted Harris pushed his way through the crowd of children mobbing Mike and grabbing the boy yelled:

"Tell them they've got to be quiet. I'm going to issue some food, then they've all got to listen to me."

Mike spoke to one of the women, and in an incredibly short space of time there was absolute silence. The woman did not say anything. She simply lifted one arm and held it above her head. The nearest children copied her, remaining silent and absolutely still. Soon there were over a hundred hands held in the air, and a quiet in which the proverbial pin could have been dropped and heard.

"You want to try that the next time we're on the parade ground," China Brown said chuckling. "That beats all your brass-throated bawling all ends up."

Ted did not reply. He had more serious things on his mind just now. He called to Curly to throw him a tin of bully beef. To Mike he said:

"I am going to show them how to open a tin. Then we'll issue one to every two children. They'll divide the meat, and they must make no noise."

Standing so that he faced the light streaming in from the cave entrance, Ted showed the children how to break off the little opener on the side of the tin, how to thread it through the little strip of metal sticking out of the side, and then how to roll the metal round the key and so divide the tin in two sections.

"Before we hand out the meat," Ted continued, "you must tell them, Mike, that I think the Germans will be here before noon. That plane wasn't flying round here just by chance. I've got a feeling that the Italian who escaped has reported us to the nearest German garrison. He'd guess we would strike inland."

"That's only guesswork, Ted," Curly Bates pointed out. "The pilot might just have been doing a routine dawn patrol."

"Don't make me laugh," Ted said coldly. "What are they going to fly dawn patrols in these hills for? I wasn't born yesterday, Curly. You can take it from me that if there's a German garrison anywhere near here they've already been told about us, which means they'll be out looking for us *pronto* . . . and that means flippin' quick."

"What am I to tell the women?" Mike asked.

"Tell them that I think the Germans will be searching this area, and that as soon as the children have eaten, we must move: march as far from here as we can."

Mike translated Ted's remarks, and everyone listened in silence until he told them the British sergeant proposed they should march from the cave just as soon as they had eaten. One of the women burst into a flood of protest, and when she had finished Mike turned to explain:

"Sergeant Harris, the women say it is not possible to walk from here to-day. The children are weak, and many of them have sore feet. Many are without footwear. If they could rest for another day or so then it might be possible to walk towards the coast."

The woman who had protested, and seemed to be in charge, took Ted by the arm and walked him to the far end of the cave. There, lying on tattered blankets were half a dozen children whose feet were roughly bandaged in rags.

"They had to be carried up the hillside," Mike explained. "Their feet were badly cut. So, you see, they cannot walk."

"I'm sorry we came here," Ted growled. "Looks as if we've brought grub *and a load of trouble.*"

He walked down to the cave entrance while Sam, China and Curly distributed tins of bully beef, and the air was filled with the chatter of excited children. To have so much meat was more like a dream than reality to them.

At the cave entrance Ted looked north along the hillside. The air was stained with the thick black smoke from the still burning plane; a funeral pall for the dead airman which would also act as a certain guide to any German troops who might be coming out to investigate.

The valleys around were thickly wooded, mostly coniferous trees, pine and larch: country which would provide good cover for anyone on the run. Ted made up his mind what to do. Calling Mike to him he said:

"Tell the women that they needn't worry about moving. Me and my men will draw off the Germans if they do start to search the area."

While the youngster was doing this, Ted called his three friends across and told them what he proposed.

"We'll have a meal, rest, and then if the Germans haven't arrived we'll strike across country and try to blow this railway viaduct. If we can do that it will give Jerry something to think about." He took the half share of a tin of bully beef which Sam Foster held out to him and was about to cut a mouthful when China Brown gave an odd little chuckle.

"What's biting you?" Ted asked irritably. He knew the signs well enough. When China laughed like that it meant he had thought of something his sergeant had overlooked.

"I just had a thought," China murmured, biting off a chunk of bully. "I remember you once told us a yarn about a bloke who caught a tiger—by the tail. The only trouble was that he daren't let go. He'd copped it right enough, but *he* was copped as well."

"Well, having said your little piece, what's on your mind?" Ted was not in the mood for joking. He hacked off a chunk of meat and popped it into his mouth.

"It's just the prisoners, that's all," China said, munching away. "What do we do with them?"

"Oh, stone the crows," Curly Bates had to slap at his chest as he almost swallowed a lump of bully beef without chewing it. "You'd forgotten them, Ted."

"I had not forgotten . . ." and there Ted stopped. Even through the excited chatter going on in the cave as the children feasted on the unaccustomed bully beef, his ears had caught a sound which rang an alarm bell at the back of his mind. Pushing past his three men he strode to the cave entrance, and now the sound was louder still: the drone of heavy aircraft.

"Sounds like a light bomber," Sam Foster said as he joined Ted. "Must be pretty close, too."

"Get back a bit," Ted ordered, and himself drew back into the entrance, while the growl of aero-engines grew thunderous. The plane, or planes, remained unseen for another minute, suggesting that the pilots were circling the peak of the very mountain in which the cave was set.

Then, so suddenly that it caused the Fighting Four to

step back even farther into the shadows, a half moon of white sailed into view, dropping steadily down towards the valley. It was followed in seconds by another, and another, until there were at least a dozen parachutists floating down.

Curly Bates rushed back into the cave and returned with three tommy-guns. He held them out.

"We could get them all," he urged, "before they land."

"Don't be a bigger fool than you can help," Ted snapped, pushing the tommy-gun aside. "We might get them all, and we might not. What we would do, we'd give away our location. Just keep back out of sight."

A few minutes later the unseen plane dropped another dozen parachutists, and it was possible to see that the men were all well armed with tommy-guns, grenades, and one of them with what looked like a walkie-talkie set. The Fighting Four lay down to watch over the rim of the cave entrance as the last of the parachutists vanished into the trees below. Two 'chutes remained visible among the dark green foliage, suggesting they had been trapped in the branches. The men would be swinging helplessly until cut down by their comrades. The roar of the unseen plane dwindled away into silence.

"Well?" Sam Foster broke the silence. "What do we do now?"

"We get out," Ted snapped, rising and striding back into the cave.

"And what about the women and children?" Curly asked, his eyes round as saucers.

"The youngsters can't walk . . . so they'll have to stay here," Ted replied. "Come on. Get your guns, ammunition, and demolition charges. Our first job is to blow that railway viaduct."

"You mean you are going to get out and leave these youngsters here?" It was China Brown, as astonished as Curly Bates.

"Yes." Ted picked up his webbing. "In case you've forgotten, there is a war on. Our orders are to blow a certain railway viaduct . . . and that is what we are going to do."

CHAPTER SEVEN

DECOY ACTION

"WE CAN'T take all this grub with us, Sergeant," this from Sam Foster. "If the Germans get in here they'll see all this, guess what has . . ."

"And take it out on the women and kids; I know," Ted interrupted. "Now stop nattering like a bunch of nit-wits. If we stay here and the Germans come we've had it . . . and the viaduct won't be blown up. Right?"

"That's right, Sarge, but . . ." China Brown began.

"All right, I want a volunteer to keep Jerry from getting into the cave," Ted said curtly. "Three of us will go and bust the railway viaduct. The volunteer will stay behind and try and keep Jerry from getting up here. All right, don't all speak at once when I ask for a volunteer. You'll do," he said pointing to Curly Bates.

"I hadn't even lifted my hand," Curly protested, adding quickly, "I was going to, but you might at least have let me volunteer."

"We can't waste time," Ted grunted, then grinned as he clapped a hand on Curly's shoulder. "Unless the Jerries bring up flame-throwers, I reckon you could keep 'em out of here for a long time, and I also reckon that in a day or two we ought to be back."

"Strike a light," Curly scoffed, "and I suppose once you get back the Jerries are bound to retreat."

"I'll recommend you for a medal when I get back," Ted chuckled, and with a wink added: "And every time we three meet after the war we'll have a drink to the memory of Curly Bates—we'll tell 'em all how brave you were."

Then, as Curly still seemed too shaken to speak, Ted went on more seriously:

"Don't be a fool, Curly. You don't think we'd leave you to fight it out alone. There's at least another half-dozen tommy-guns here. There's plenty of ammo. You've got six women here who, unless I'm sadly mistaken, will fight like Kilkenny cats; but, in any case, I'm hoping you won't have to fight at all. We're going to try to draw the Jerries away. If we can do that your job will be to see that everything is ready for a quick move when we get back."

"Move?"

"Of course. We're not going to leave these women and youngsters here to starve. There's a boat coming to take us off, isn't there, in a few days' time. If we can get this lot down to the coast . . . okay, they can be shipped across to Italy."

Ted explained to Mike what he planned, and asked the youngster if any of the women spoke English. One knew a little of the language, and she was told that Curly would stay with them. If Ted's plan to draw the Germans off did not work, they were to try to hold the cave as long as possible. Ted, Sam, and China Brown would come back the moment they had blown the railway viaduct, and if the battle was still going on would do something about it.

"Three men will do something about it," the woman

queried, frowning. "How can three men do this?"

Mike could only shrug. He did not know, but they were in a cleft stick, and it seemed the British sergeant meant to do his job first. Once the viaduct was blown he would be free to think about the women and children.

"It is war," Mike said sadly. "If the Germans are defeated all will be well."

"If the Germans get into this cave," the woman said sadly, "we shall all die. They will shoot us as Partisans and then the children will starve."

Two minutes later Ted, Sam and China Brown slipped out of the cave and hurried to the nearest boulders to avoid being spotted from the valley. Then they began to make their way downhill.

To have gone directly downhill would have been asking for trouble. Although there was no sign of life, except for the two white splashes of parachute silk in the trees, the Germans who had been dropped by plane were unlikely to be sitting around. German paratroopers, like their British counterparts, were usually tough, well-seasoned troops.

In view of this Ted, Sam and China moved diagonally across the face of the hill, dodging from cover to cover, and so getting as far out of the direct line between valley and cave as possible. Finally they rounded a shoulder of the hill, and for the moment could not see the two parachutes.

"Well, reckon we can make a bit of speed now, eh, Sarge," China suggested. "I reckon we're out of sight here."

"Famous last words, my lad," Ted hooted sarcastically. "Ever hear of the flippin' ostrich? It hides its head in the sand, so they say, and reckons if it can't see anything, nobody can see it. You'll just keep going from cover to cover until I say different."

It proved to be a very wise precaution, for five minutes later Sam Foster caught sight of a German coming up the hill almost directly beneath them. It proved one thing, the Germans did not know where the cave was, and were encircling the hill so as to cut off any escape route.

"We'll wait for him," Ted decided, and with a grin added: "Reckon he'll get an Iron Cross, First Class, when he reports being the first to contact the Britishers."

Ten minutes later the German paratrooper drew near. He was well-armed with an automatic weapon, a pistol and two grenades. Round his neck hung a whistle, an instrument he never had the chance to use.

Sam Foster brought the man down. The Britisher was so well concealed that the German actually walked past the rock behind which Sam was hidden. It must have given the man a terrific shock when, turning to discover what had made a slight sound to his right—Sam had tossed a pebble to distract the German's attention—a shadow seemed to grow from the very ground just behind him.

Sam's methods would have looked too simple to an onlooker. His left arm went round the man's chest, pinning his arms, his right hand cuffed the back of the coal-scuttle helmet, sending it forward and over the German's face, yet not so far over that it fell off. At the same time the Britisher's right foot kicked smartly at the German's right ankle, so that he tripped and went face down.

As the man fell Sam released him, and a moment later had his knee in the small of his victim's back while the muzzle of his tommy-gun pressed hard against the back of the unprotected neck. It was a very slick demonstration of unarmed combat.

A few moments later Ted and China arrived. They turned the man over and removed his coal-scuttle helmet. Beyond the loss of a little skin scraped from the end of his nose by his own helmet, the German was uninjured; but he was a very frightened man. His expression was one of fear and horror, as if he half expected to be killed within the next second or so.

"Tie his wrists and ankles," Ted ordered, moving away to a vantage point where he could watch yet be unseen.

"Want a whistle, Ted?" China asked a few moments later, and tossed over the whistle on a plaited lanyard which he had taken from around the prisoner's neck. "Be just the thing to stick in the stocking of one of your nephews next Christmas. Save you a bob or so in presents."

Ted grinned and was about to slip the souvenir into his pocket when a thought struck him and a sudden wary look came into his eyes. He stared at the whistle for a moment then tossed it back saying:

"No, keep it, China." But he tossed it short so that it was out of reach of China Brown, and as the latter reached out to pick it up Ted waved a hand, a silent signal to leave the whistle on the ground.

Then, walking across, he elbowed China aside, saying:

"I'll do the tying-up."

Just for a moment a look of annoyance showed on China's face, but it was gone in an instant. Ted Harris never did anything without reason, and he knew that when it came to tying knots China was no duffer. China and Sam Foster exchanged glances as they watched their sergeant truss the German's wrists. He was not following the usual method.

In the past, when they had any reason to secure a prisoner, they tied his hands behind his back, then tied a rope from his wrists to his ankles, that prevented him getting to his feet, or even sitting up. Ted, for some reason, was merely tying the German's wrists.

"Okay, let's go," Ted had finished his job. He slung the German Schmeisser over his left shoulder, stuffed the magazines of ammunition into his belt then tossed the two German grenades across, one to Sam, the other to China. For the first time since setting foot on Yugoslav soil, Sergeant Ted Harris seemed to be enjoying himself.

He led his two friends diagonally across the hillside until they were about sixty yards from the spot where they had left their prisoner, making sure that they did not expose themselves at all during the process.

When they got to a cluster of rocks he stopped and, cocking the Schmeisser after making sure the magazine was full, he winked at China, then at Sam.

"Go on, ask me," he taunted. "Why didn't I let you finish tying him up, and why didn't I do the usual job of linking his wrists to his ankles."

"He's like a kid with a new toy, isn't he," China jeered. "He thinks he's done something smart and he wants to tell us about it. Go on, Sam, ask him. It'll spoil his fun if he can't brag."

"Well, at least I had the savvy to realise something you hadn't noticed," Ted growled. "That whistle. If I hadn't been there you'd have stuffed it into your pocket wouldn't you? Go on, admit it, you would."

"I expect I would," China agreed. "So what. You've left it lying near the Jerry. Does it win the flippin' war for us? There must be a reason. Okay, I'll buy it."

"He wasn't wearing a whistle in case he got lost," Ted said soberly now. "It was, unless I'm badly mistaken, so that he could signal to the others. How many were there? About two dozen? Okay. They've been dropped here to make sure the Commandos didn't get away . . . before reinforcements arrived. I'll bet you my last shirt . . ."

"Don't bet that, Sarge," and for the first time Sam Foster was grinning widely. "You've already bet your last shirt button and lost it. Bet something else."

"Okay, I'll bet drinks all round when we get back that these Jerries have agreed on some system of signalling . . . they're probably spreading out round the base of this mountain. They're hoping that if the 'enemy,' that's us, tries to get away then one of their blokes will see the move. He whistles . . . calls up the others. Get the idea, boys?"

"Yeah, I can see it working," China admitted. "But why leave him to get free and leave him his whistle? Are we not supposed to win?"

"This is how we do win, if the thing works out how

I'm hoping it will. When that Jerry gets free enough to get the whistle to his mouth he'll call up the others .... and if you will take a gander back where we came from, any reinforcements coming to that bloke will be in full view of us."

Sam and China turned and peeping, round their rocky cover, saw that what Ted had just told them was the truth. Anyone coming up to their prisoner would be in full view.

"Okay, the drinks are on me," Sam Foster said ruefully. "I reckon I ought to have known."

Ted spat on his hands and grinned. Then they sat and waited. Five minutes went by. Ten minutes, and still there was neither sign nor sound from their prisoner.

"Mebbe I was wrong," Ted finally murmured. "Hard luck, and we've wasted a lot of time. Come on, we'll . . ."

"Pheep-pheep-pheep . . . pheep-pheep . . . pheep . . . pheep."

At the first shrill "pheep" Ted Harris flung himself down, followed by Sam and China. They eased themselves into positions where they could see the cluster of boulders among which they had left their prisoner. For five minutes the whistling continued, keeping to the same signal pattern. Then from somewhere on the shoulder of the mountain—and it could not have been very far from the cave where the Yugoslav children were hiding—came a single long blast.

"That's it," Ted sounded triumphant. "Now, Sam, you've got that bloke's Schmeisser. Fire one or two short bursts, then a long one, then we'll scram."

Sam did as ordered, and the familiar chack-chack-chack of the German Schmeisser automatic brought back faint echoes from other mountains. When he had finished his magazine Sam turned for further instructions.

"I said we'd scram now," Ted repeated. "That's all I wanted—an answer from the other Jerries."

They crawled about eighty yards until they came to the lip of a shallow ravine. A mountain rill tumbled and splashed down the centre of it, and the three Britishers were glad to pause for a few moments to drink deep of the icy, refreshing water. Sam took the opportunity to ask why he should fire when there was no one in sight.

"China knows," Ted chuckled, winking. "That's why he doesn't ask. Tell him, China."

China Brown, splashing water on to his dirty face, looked up for a moment then wiping his nose with the back of his hand said:

"Sam, I've given over asking why Ted does things. Most times they strike me as daft . . . thought I knew him, but I don't. If you want to know why we're doing these cuckoo stunts—ask the Brains, Sergeant Edward Harris, M.C. He might know. Sometimes he does."

"He knows all the time, China my lad," Ted growled, "and you know he knows. Sam, we've two important things to do. Bust that flippin' railway viaduct, and then get back to pick up Curly Bates . . . and the kids."

Sam nodded agreement. He knew that.

"We've got to keep the Jerries away from the caves," Ted went on. "What do you think the rest of those perishing parachutists are going to do when they hear one of their pals whistling for help . . . then hear his Schmeisser rattling? Come on, Sam, use your nut."

"Well, if I was one of them I'd hurry to lend a hand," Sam suggested.

"That's what the Jerries are doing," Ted explained. "And when we get lower down this hillside we're going to do some more firing. We kid the Jerries that we're not in the cave at all . . . but on the run, see. Draw 'em away."

"Clever!" Sam agreed.

"You keep saying things like that to him, Sam, and Ted'll be giving you one of his stripes," China jeered. "Come on, before I start telling lies and saying you are a big handsome soldier."

"When we get back to Italy, remind me to take you round the back of the barracks to give you a thick ear." Ted slapped China playfully across the shoulders. "Come on."

They hurried down the ravine, Ted Harris in the lead, China bringing up the rear. Their tommy-guns were cocked, and they halted every two or three minutes to listen. When they had dropped about six hundred feet nearer the trees fringing the foot of the mountain, Ted ordered Sam to load the German Schmeisser again, fire a short burst, then fire a longer burst after Ted had rattled off a few rounds from his tommy-gun.

There was a definite difference in the sounds made by the two automatics, and Ted was hoping it would give the impression to anyone who heard the quick bursts of shots, that a running battle was in progress.

"We want to draw that bunch off the mountain," Ted explained, re-loading. "If we can get 'em away, and following us towards the railway, I think Curly and the kids should be safe."

The ravine began to widen out, and the gurgling rivulet was joined by several others until it broadened out to become a fast-flowing stream some twenty yards wide. As the ravine flattened out rapidly to a shallow valley, trees and shrubs appeared, and with the smoother going Ted was able to set a faster pace.

Sam put his foot on a round stone which rolled under him and he went down with a crash. Ted and China stopped, afraid he might have twisted an ankle, and as they picked up his tommy-gun and helped him to his feet there came a thin, appealing cry from behind them. It made them turn and look back the way they had come.

"Sam . . . Sam . . . Wait for me. S A M!"

"That's the kid . . . Mike!" Ted Harris growled, hardly able to believe his ears. "For pete's sake what's he chasing us for?"

Sam wiped his nose with the back of his hand, removing a piece of wet mud sticking to the end of it. Then, as he was about to turn and look back to see if he could make out the young Yugoslav, his sensitive ears picked out another, quite different sound. He cupped a hand about his left ear, a startled expression on his face.

"What's the matter?" Ted asked.

"I can hear a motor."

Ted and China cupped hands about their ears, but a few seconds elapsed before China nodded.

"He's right, Ted. I can just hear it."

"Sam!" Mike was in sight now, and still yelled despairingly. Ted held his arms high, then put his hands to his mouth, signalling for the boy to be silent. His action must have been understood for there were no more calls, and the boy, his right knee bleeding as a result of a fall in the stream farther up the valley, stumbled nearer, obviously almost exhausted by his wild dash.

"I . . . I've . . . come to . . . guide you," he gasped. "Trici said you would need . . ."

"Ted," Sam interrupted urgently, "that motor sounds nearer. Suppose it is a tank!"

"Oh, no," China protested. "Not a flippin' tank."

"All right, kid, don't tell us now," Ted quietened Mike's gasping explanations of why he had followed them. He looked round with the eye of an expert for some place where they could get under cover; but they were in a difficult position. The ravine had levelled out considerably. The ground was flattening, and the only cover was that provided by an occasional tree or shrub, and some upthrusting slabs of rock. To climb out of the valley might be disastrous, since the approaching vehicle might well be on the hillside, and not in the valley at all.

"What about the river?" China asked, frowning at the smooth, flowing water which he knew to be very cold.

"No!" Ted turned down the suggestion at once. "Too shallow. We'd have to lie flat and we might still be seen. Y'know, I didn't expect Jerry to be so quick off the mark. Parachutists--yes. Though they were here a darn sight quicker than I imagined. I'm pretty sure, now, that this spot of bother comes from letting that Italian get away."

"I'm sorry, Sarge," Sam Foster looked very worried.

"Not your fault," Ted told him. "It isn't often a bloke gets away from us, but that Eyetie knew his onions, and I think he belted across to the nearest Jerry headquarters, told them Commandos had landed, and this is the result. The Jerries must be pretty nervous to turn out troops like this. They must have had parachutists standing by even before they sent off that Fieseler Storch, and they must have started mechanised troops off as well."

Ted was right, for that was exactly what the Germans had done, and was the reason why they were here so quickly.

"We'd better do something," China Brown said. "They'll be here any minute now."

"Next thing you'll be telling me Queen Victoria's dead," Ted growled. "Come on. No use waiting for 'em. We'll go down and see who they are. Safety catches off, and let me fire first."

He led the way at a crouching run towards where the valley took a sharp turn to the right. The roar of engines was much louder now, and when they were within twenty yards of a big buttress of rock which formed the "corner" in the valley, a German half-track troop carrier rattled into view. A German officer sat beside the driver; behind them and facing each other, were sixteen soldiers, each nursing a rifle between his knees.

Germans and British saw each other at exactly the

same moment; but the German officer was in a much better position for shooting than Ted Harris. He had a Schmeisser lying across where the windshield should have been, so that he could blast off a score of shots by simply squeezing the trigger. His safety catch was in the *"off"* position, and within seconds of seeing the three Britishers he was firing:

Chack-a-chack-a-chacka-chacka-chacka!

He should have dropped Ted, Sam and China in their tracks, and would have finished all three there and then if his driver had not been an expert. Acting on the spur of the moment the driver dropped his foot on his right hand clutch, putting the right hand track out of action at once.

The result was that the vehicle spun round as adroitly as any ballet dancer, the left hand track grinding away and turning them in a ninety-degree turn in seconds. The result was that the savage burst of fire from the officer's Schmeisser sprayed lead just to the left of Ted, Sam and China, and then over a wide field of fire . . . in which there was not a living target.

Ted Harris did not stretch his luck any further. He dropped to one knee and his tommy-gun ripped out a stream of lead.

Tat-tat-tat-tat-tat-tat-tat!

The goddess of Luck must have been smiling on Ted when he fired that first short burst. Not only was his shooting accurate enough to put driver and officer out of action, but the sudden sharp swerve of the vehicle stopped the sixteen men in her from doing anything to hit back. They were accustomed to rough rides, but had not been expecting such a swift, ninety-degree turn. They were thrown off-balance, and, before they could recover, another burst of shots whistled over their head.

In almost the same moment the vehicle came to a sudden stop. On these half track vehicles, where the steering is done by de-clutching one of the tracks, the throttle is hand operated. The last thing the driver did before he slumped forward was to close the throttle, and a moment later the engine stalled.

For perhaps five seconds Death hung in the air. Sixteen soldiers looked over the back of the vehicle, and faced three grim-faced Britishers each with a tommy-gun in his hands. Smoke was curling from the muzzle of Ted's weapon. At the least sign of resistance there would have been a chattering roar from three guns, and most if not all the sixteen men would have been either killed or badly wounded.

An N.C.O. raised his hands. He was no coward, but this was one of those times in war when resistance meant death. His example was followed by the other fifteen. Sam stepped to one side, China to the other, so they could cover the troop-carrier while Ted went nearer. The Germans were left with only one thing to do, and they did it, surrendering without a fight.

There was a hard clatter of metal on metal as rifle after rifle was dropped on to the floor of the troop-carrier. One by one the men scrambled over the back. One by one they dropped the stick bombs which had been looped to their belts. They were well equipped for an assault, and were moving up to support the paratroopers dropped an hour earlier.

Young Mike, eyes like saucers, had gone to the front of the troop-carrier to keep an eye on the driver and the officer. Neither of the men showed any signs of resistance. Ted's crippling burst of fire had put them out of action for some time to come.

"Anybody speak English?" Ted asked, when the prisoners were lined up. One man gave a little start, but shook his head emphatically when Ted asked him if he did. "Doesn't matter," the British sergeant said coldly. "Just in case anybody does I'll give you a word of advice. If you've got a white rag of any kind . . . get it out and be ready to wave it in case any more of our men come down."

It was obvious then that at least two of the sixteen understood English, for they looked nervously round, as if half expecting to see more dirty-faced commandos coming down the valley.

"You'll take your boots off," Ted began, and grinned as one of the two men who had looked round when asked if anyone spoke English, immediately bent down to begin taking off his boots. "Tell the others."

In the next minute or so sixteen men piled their boots in a heap. Sam and Mike carried them to the banks of the stream and threw them in, where they disappeared, some tossing gently like boats, others turning over and filling in a few seconds.

While this was happening, China superintended the removal of the two injured men. They were laid on the grass and China indicated that they could be given first aid. When Sam and Mike returned from getting rid of the boots, Ted climbed into the driving seat and re-started the engine.

He sat for a moment or so, with both tracks out of gear, then put one track in gear and swung the troop-carrier round until it was facing down the valley. Sam piled the rifles and the stick bombs into the back of the carrier. Then helped Mike aboard. China got into the front with Ted.

"Tell 'em, Sam, not to forget their white flag. They had better keep close together for the next hour, just in case any other parties of commandos pass this way."

Sam frowned, but repeated what Ted had just told him. That the message was well understood was obvious from what happened. Two of the Germans began tying white handkerchiefs together while the others, hands still held high, began nervously looking up the valley.

Ted let in his clutches and with a clatter the troop-carrier began to move down the valley.

"I don't see the reason for all this talk about other commandos knocking around," China Brown said as he changed Ted's tommy-gun magazine for a full one. "I suppose it'll keep 'em hanging about, but they wouldn't get far anyway, not having boots."

"I want word to get to Jerry headquarters that there are a lot of us in the region," Ted pointed out. "If they think there are only one or two, they may well search the mountain, find the cave, and that would be the end of Curly Bates, the women and the youngsters. If they think we've moved off the mountain . . . okay, Curly will still be sitting pretty when we get back."

"You mean *if* we get back," China growled. "You know, I've got a feeling, Ted, that things have gone too smoothly for us this morning. We shoot that spotter plane down, we get away with this car . . . luck like that can't last."

"I was born under a lucky star," Ted shouted back. "It's better to be born lucky than to be born rich . . . and I know I wasn't born rich."

While Sam squatted in the back of the troop-carrier, his tommy-gun across his knees, young Mike leaned over the front so that he could answer any questions Ted might ask. The boy knew the region well, since he had been poaching and stealing food for the children throughout the area for the past ten months.

They came into the beginning of the woodland, and Mike was in the midst of explaining to Ted that a rough track started a hundred yards or so away to the right, a track which ran down to the mile-distant railway-crossing, and so on to a reasonably good road, when a German soldier walked out into the glade ahead of them.

He stood waving them down, quite unconcerned, and obviously sure that the men in the troop-carrier were Germans like himself. Ted never slackened speed in the least and at the last moment the German seemed to realise that he had made a mistake. He gave a startled yelp and flinging himself to one side began to run.

Ted stamped hard on his right hand clutch, moment-arily stopping the track on that side and causing the vehicle to make a quick half turn to the right. He started in pursuit of the German, only to change his mind within seconds. Not more than fifty yards ahead of him were two more troop-carrying half-tracks, and standing about, smoking and talking were some fifty or more troops.

It was impossible to tell what the startled German was yelling, but the effect was immediate. Men grabbed for weapons, men ran for shelter, an officer struggled to open his pistol holster.

It was in that moment, when anything could happen, that Sam Foster did the right thing. He whipped out the safety pins of two of the German stick bombs which lay in the bottom of the carrier, and tossed them out, one on either side, then he yelled to Ted and China to duck.

The whole incident began and ended within forty seconds. Soldiers grabbed for rifles and Schmeissers. The troop-carrier ran right through the glade, scattering Germans to left and right. Already one of the crew of a troop-carrier was starting his engine. Then the stick bombs went off:

Crump . . .crump!

CHAPTER EIGHT

HARE—AND HOUNDS

THERE WERE two flashes of yellow-red fire as the stick bombs went off. They seemed more brilliant because the halting place for the Germans was in the shade of some giant oak trees.

Sam threw his bombs then dragged Mike down below the level of the armour-plated sides of the vehicle. It was as well that he did, for no sooner was the glade lit up by the flash than it sounded as if a devil's tattoo was being played by giant hammers on the truck sides.

There were yells of fear and one or two of pain from the Germans as most of them flung themselves down. The man in the driving seat of the farthest of the two troop-carriers ought to have earned at least an Iron Cross Second Class, for he swung his vehicle round within seconds of the explosions and started it in pursuit. Another German, who had grabbed a rifle a few seconds before throwing himself to the ground, sent three rounds of very rapid, and fairly accurate fire after the Britishers. His second bullet drove through the back of the troop-carrier as if it had been nothing stronger than plywood. The bullet went past Sam Foster's ear with that frightening moan peculiar to a bullet which is ricochetting and battered out of shape.

Sam sent a short burst back in the hope of dampening

the enthusiasm of anyone thinking of pursuit, and a few moments later Ted was out on the rough track Mike had been speaking of.

It was a very rough track. Parts which were obviously soft spots in wet weather had been strengthened by having branches of trees dropped in them, and the troop-carrier bumped and bounced appallingly whenever it crossed one of these patches.

"How are we doing?" Ted yelled a minute or so later. "Nobody hurt?"

"I'm all right," Sam yelled back, "but you'd better get your foot down, I think one of their troop-carriers is following us."

"I hope it's full of Jerries," was Ted's reply. "They won't half have a joyride if they come along here at speed."

Had there not been a definite track through the woods no progress would have been possible, for now they were passing through a patch of conifers, larch, pine and fir. These trees grew so close, and their wide-spreading lower branches were so low that it was impossible for anything on four wheels to get through.

The track wound this way and that for some distance, then quite suddenly became as straight as a ruler. That brought danger. The moment the first German vehicle came into the straight, the men in her began to shoot. Pin-points of light flickered in the gloom, and with the first burst, three bullets ripped into the metal of the truck, making the half-track jump a little under the impact.

Sam lifted his tommy-gun, then decided not to fire back. The track was so bumpy that it was impossible to aim accurately, and in any case tommy-guns were not made for anything but relatively close-quarter work.

More pin-points of light, but this time only one bullet drew a "clang" from the fleeing troop-carrier. Sam lifted his head for a second to see where they were going, and frowned as he realised they were rapidly coming out of the wood. The Germans would have an advantage now, for they could halt at the fringe of the trees and keeping under cover, take careful aim at the fugitives.

"I'm going to leave a little present for them, Ted," he yelled. "A grenade. Okay?"

"The quicker the better," Ted roared. "Mike says the railway-crossing isn't so far from here, and there's probably a telephone there. I'd like to stop for a minute and put it out of action."

Sam dropped his grenade carefully over the back and counted seven. He grunted in disgust when he saw the flash as it exploded. Hitting the hard ground the grenade had unfortunately bounced to one side. Sam hurriedly dropped another grenade and reinforced it with two German stick bombs.

Then, quite suddenly, they were out of the gloom and into the sunlight. Behind them the tall conifers looked like a mighty wall, dark at the base and hard green where the foliage was catching the sunlight.

Crack . . . crack . . . crack! Faintly above the roar of the troop-carrier's engine came the sound of the triple explosions, and this time two of the bombs were in the middle of the track.

Sam watched anxiously, hoping that the first of the German troop-carriers would be so near when the grenades and stick bombs went off that they would catch at least some of the shrapnel.

He was disappointed, for seconds after the flashes had died away the first troop-carrier nosed cautiously round on the outside of the track. The only gain had been a few seconds of time.

"They're still coming," Sam yelled, and decided to risk a short burst from his tommy-gun. He grunted in disgust when he saw the spurts of dust nearly thirty yards ahead of the first troop-carrier. A jolt had made him drop his muzzle and his bullets had been short ranged.

Ted Harris did not even shoot a glance over his shoulder to see what was happening. The fact that Sam Foster was being driven to fire at their pursuers told him the Germans were not being left behind and might even be gaining on them. He jazzed the accelerator, thinking that perhaps he was not getting all the juice to his engine it needed, but it made no difference.

"This could be sticky, China," he shouted. "If there's a siding or a level-crossing keeper's cottage ahead, we ought to cut the wires, and so stop the Jerries from getting word to anybody ahead."

China half rose in his seat to look behind and shook his head as he slumped back by the side of Ted.

"I think they're gaining on us," he yelled. "If we could find a spot . . ." and there he stopped. From somewhere ahead had come the long, mournful hoot of a locomotive whistle. There could only be one reason for an engine-driver whistling out here, and that was to warn anyone who might be near the level-crossing.

"Keep your fingers crossed and say your prayers,"

Ted shouted, hunching even more over the controls. "If that is a train coming along the line . . . we could be unlucky."

Less than a minute later they swung round a bend in the road, and the forest virtually stopped. Ahead of them was a patch of land which had been cleared of trees, and across it they could see not only a cottage with telephone poles beyond it, but a stretch of railway line, on which a long train was moving.

"You'd better say another prayer, China," Ted shouted. "I'm going to try and get across."

"You'll never do it," China warned, and half turning shouted to Sam in the back: "Sam, better get ready to jump."

Sam turned and stared, his eyes narrowing as he saw the giant locomotive rolling nearer and nearer the level-crossing. Behind it was a long string of flats and box-cars. The speed of the train was probably no more than 18 miles an hour, but it would be a miracle if Ted beat the locomotive to the level-crossing.

The driver must have seen the racing troop-carrier, for he reached for his whistle lever and sent two jets of steam into the air as he sounded a warning *toot-tooo-oot*. Young Mike got to his feet, hanging on to the side of the vehicle, and his eyes were wide with terror.

In about twenty seconds, which seemed ten times as long to China, Sam and Mike, Ted Harris covered the distance which separated them from the crossing. In that same time the driver of the locomotive grabbed for his air brakes, making a last-minute move to avoid a crash.

His big driving wheels threw off sparks as they

skidded along the rails, but the box-cars and flats were not connected for vacuum braking, so they kept on pushing, and the engine slithered on to the level-crossing, closing it far more effectively than any man-made gates.

China swung up his hands to protect his face. Sam Foster dropped to his knees and braced himself for the crash.

Crunch!

There would have been a devastating crash if the troop-carrier had been any ordinary wheeled vehicle; but at the very last moment Ted Harris, realising he could not beat the big loco, stamped his foot hard down on the clutch pedal of the left-hand track. That stopped, but the right-hand track kept running and swung the troop-carrier round almost on its axis.

The side of the vehicle crunched heavily against a seven-foot driving wheel and sparks flew on all sides. China Brown leapt out, a split second after, Ted and Sam Foster went over the side just as the troop-carrier began to turn over.

In the next five seconds the three Britishers gave a perfect demonstration of their readiness for any emergency. Mike screamed as the troop-carrier began to overturn. Sam hit the rutted dirt track, spun round and, grabbing the boy, somehow managed to leap back in time to avoid being struck by the vehicle.

China Brown and Ted Harris never even looked round at the scream. They had absolute confidence in Sam being able to deal with that side of the business. They dropped flat and a moment later were sending streams of bullets at the approaching Germans.

There was no jolting vehicle to upset their aim, and within seconds the first troop-carrier had jerked to a stop. The second one bumped into it. Then Germans spewed out, diving for cover.

The train, its wheels still screeching under locked brake shoes, jolted on, box-car after box-car rolling over the level crossing, but at a reducing speed.

"Hold 'em, China," Ted bawled. "I'm going to get the train going again. Then you must get aboard. We can't stay and fight it out."

The first return fire from the Germans was now coming over, bullets spanging against the metal sides of the box-cars. Ted leapt to his feet and raced alongside the train. The driver and his fireman were both leaning from their cab, looking down the track, and wondering what was happening. They recognised the troop-carrier which had hit them as being of German make. Yet the occupants of it were acting very strangely. They were firing at two other German troop-carriers.

Then Ted appeared, smoking tommy-gun in his right hand. He presented a grim picture. Unwashed and unshaven, his face still dirtied from the boot-black camouflage put on before they left Italy, he was fierce-looking enough to frighten almost anyone.

The driver reached for his fireman's shovel, but changed his mind as Ted gave his trigger a light touch and sent three bullets whistling over the cab. By now the locked brakes had brought the long train almost to a stop. Ted scrambled up the iron-runged steps into the cab, the Yugoslav fireman and driver backing away, fear in their eyes.

"English . . . English," Ted yelled, scrambling on to the footplate and waving the smoking tommy-gun. "Drive . . . on . . . savvy, on," and he pointed to the regulator.

"Ingleesi!" the driver repeated, a look of incredible amazement in his eyes. Then he spun the little brass wheel which controlled the Westinghouse air brakes. The big locomotive ceased shuddering as the driving wheels came unlocked. A few moments later there was a "chuff-chuff" from the smoke-stack as steam went into the fat cylinders again.

Ted went to the left-hand side and looked down the track. He ducked instinctively as something "spanged" against the engine tender. The Germans were firing at the engine as well as at China, Sam and Mike.

A few moments later Mike came bounding along the track, holding out his hands. The train, moving at five or six miles an hour, was slowly beginning to pick up speed again. Ted scrambled down the engine ladder, caught Mike's outstretched right hand. Then with a smooth upward jerk he lifted the boy off his feet. Mike swung his left hand to the tarnished brass rail alongside the ladder, and was safe.

Back at the level crossing Sam and China were firing occasional bursts at the Germans, and being forced to keep as low as possible because of the blistering fire being directed at them. There was a continuous "whang-clang-tung" from the trucks as bullets smacked against them, but now the wheels were starting to roll by a little quicker.

"Scram," China yelled. "Duck between the cars and you'll be hidden at once."

"And you?"

"Don't worry about me, pal," China bawled. "I've a lot of back pay owing to me and I don't intend to lose it." He slammed the last spare magazine into the German Schmeisser, fired a short burst, swinging the muzzle in an arc so as to give the Germans the full benefit of it. He shot a quick glance behind, saw that Sam was running alongside the track. He saw him dodge between two cars then China emptied his magazine.

The Germans had deployed into a line some sixty yards long, and they were keeping low. A few seconds elapsed after China emptied his magazine before there was any reply. Then came a steady crash of fire. The Germans were firing in turn to keep their foe with his head down.

A man fired a short burst, then he jumped up and ran a dozen yards before throwing himself full length again. In this way they could keep up an almost unbroken fire and yet advance.

China was lying as close to the earth as possible. Only the fact that the side of the track was lower than the ground was saving him. The situation was growing more and more desperate, for the train was gradually picking up speed, and if he did not get aboard very soon his chance of escape would be gone.

He unhooked one of the German stick bombs looped to his belt. Making sure that his own tommy-gun was safely looped over his left shoulder, he took a quick glance behind him at the box-car wheels as they clacked over the rails.

"Well, for better or for worse, as they say at weddings," he muttered. "It's now or never, China," and he tossed the stick bomb as far as he could in the direction of the advancing Germans. He counted six, then turned and sprinted the three yards which separated him from the line, dropping face down within a foot of the grinding wheels.

Bang! The stick bomb went off, and the result was exactly as China hoped. Every German ducked. China got to his feet and running a few yards along with the train, slipped in between two of the cars. For one moment he thought he was going to fall. His battle-dress sleeve caught on the end of a bolt sticking out from the box-car and partially threw him off-balance.

With a yelp of dismay, dragged out of him by the shock, China leaped for the buffers. They were not touching, for the couplings were at full stretch. He got across them, arms and head over one side, legs hanging over the other.

"Tat-tat-tat-tat-tat-tatatatatata" There was an absolute fusillade of Schmeisser fire, but China had timed his flight perfectly. Only two bullets came near enough to make him cringe. They struck the metalwork of the truck ahead and ricochetted off with weird moans, leaving white splashes of lead on the rusted iron plating.

"And the best of British luck to the lot of you," China grunted, looking ruefully at the knuckles of his left hand. In the mad scramble to get aboard he had knocked his hand on a bolt head and torn off a patch of skin. He licked the bleeding spot, then spat out the taste of dirt and blood.

As he fought to get on top of the swaying box-car he muttered to himself:

"China, my boy, it's about time you got back to Blighty for a spot of leave, or something. I reckon your luck is beginning to run out. We don't seem to be doing as well as we have in the past."

When he finally got on top of the swaying coach, and had rested for a minute or so to get back his breath, he looked over the rest of the box-cars in the direction of the level-crossing. He was surprised to note that it was much nearer than he had imagined it would be.

"Luvvaduck, the flippin' train isn't doin' more than a crawl." It was actually doing about ten miles an hour, but was losing even that speed. The big engine, its valve gear old, its cylinder heads long in need of new packing, was making very slow work of a gradient.

If the Germans had made a determined attempt to catch up with it, and board it, they could have done so, for the speed dropped until, when it reached the top of the gradient, it was crawling along at no more than five miles an hour.

China's first intention had been to move along the box-car tops and join Ted, Sam and young Mike in the engine cab; but there was something which made him move in the opposite direction. Coming along the track, and making heavy weather of the trip, were two of the German half-tracks.

When the train was going at its slowest, China discouraged the Germans from approaching closer by firing a couple of short bursts at them, kicking up the dust within a dozen yards of the nearest vehicle and causing her crew to get out in a hurry and dive for shelter by the track side.

It took the long train more than half an hour to cover six miles, and in that time the Germans had been busy. Both half-track vehicles were equipped with radio and the officer in charge was quickly in contact with his headquarters in Cavtat. He told them the train was in the hands of British commandos, and urged that troops should be sent to meet the train—possibly to stop it at some convenient point—so that the Commandos could be brought to bay and disposed of.

After getting to the top of the gradient the engine, puffing mightily, and with clouds of steam gushing from its leaky cylinders, slowly began to gather speed. The German vehicles were being left behind, and China decided he could risk making a dash to the engine cab to see what was happening there.

By the time he got to the front of the train, he was growing quite confident in his jumps from one box-car to the next, and was grinning when he finally leaped across to the coal tender and from there slithered down on to the footplate.

He gave Ted, Sam and Mike the news that two German troop-carrying cars had been chasing them.

"I think I saw them off," he said, winking at Sam. "Two quick bursts from the old pea-shooter and they were diving for cover like half-baked rabbits."

"Fine," Ted said, fishing out a spare tommy-gun magazine. "Here you are, take this and make sure they don't creep up on us. If we strike another gradient, this old engine may give up the ghost."

"Go back . . . along all those flippin' box-cars?"

China croaked. "Cor, you don't half like makin' me work overtime don't you. If I . . . oh, ta," and he grinned his thanks as the Yugoslav engine-driver offered him a bottle and motioned him to drink.

"Don't drown yourself," Ted warned, a twinkle in his eyes. "Yugoslav wine is pretty strong stuff they tell me."

"I'll risk it," China said, wiping the mouth of the bottle with a hand which was so dirty it was hardly possible to see the colour of his skin. "They reckon you don't know a country until you've drunk its wine. Cheers!"

"Cheers," Ted echoed, and burst out laughing as China took a deep swig from the bottle, swallowed, then stared at the engine-driver with a look of disgust and hurt dignity on his face.

"What's the matter? Don't you like cold tea?" Sam Foster asked, grinning. "We thought it would be wine, too, so you aren't the only one who's been taken in."

"Cold tea!" China muttered disgustedly, but he lifted the bottle and drained it. Then handed it back to its owner saying: "Thanks, pal. I've heard before that cold tea is the best drink for engine-drivers . . . well, it's pretty good stuff when you're thirsty."

As he turned to clamber on to the tender top, Ted called after him.

"If I want you down here again, I'll fire a couple of shots. If we stop the train it means get off. Okay."

"Okay," and China went back along the length of the train, swaying this way and that as if he had been walking box-cars travelling at nearly twenty miles an hour all his life.

When he got to the end car, with a diminutive guards van bumping and rolling at the very end of the train, the two German troop-carriers were no more than a hundred yards distant.

"Come any nearer and I'll give you a bellyful of lead," China threatened, lying down so that he would not present himself as an easy target. He lay like that for almost quarter of an hour, then, from the front of the long train, came five long blasts on the engine whistle. China stiffened. That was obviously a signal, but Ted had not mentioned anything about using the train whistle as a signal. The five blasts cut the air again, and then the train began to slow down.

At almost the same moment the monotonous clack-clack-clacketty-clack of wheels going over rail junctions which had been given too little attention since the war began, changed. The sound became a dull roar, causing China to look towards the track side.

His eyes widened. They were starting to cross a viaduct; it was a narrow ribbon of a bridge, with only one set of tracks. Even China, who knew nothing about bridges or railway engineering could see that the brickwork was in need of attention. When he looked beyond the crumbling parapet, however, he had a sudden cold feeling around his stomach.

He could see down into a deep valley. To him it looked hundreds of feet deep—actually it was 150 feet at its deepest point. In its day, the viaduct must have been a triumph of engineering skill, for it was a quarter of a mile long.

The engine whistle was screaming again as the train crawled, ever more slowly, towards the centre of the bridge. Finally it came to a stop. China Brown's end of the train was about a hundred yards from the beginning of the bridge, and the two troop-carriers, the Germans huddled low, halted at the beginning of the bridge. Then they backed away and the men dismounted.

"If you want to see to-morrow, chums, you won't come any nearer," China murmured, cocking his tommy-gun and pushing the safety catch to the "*off*" position. "You walk on to this bridge and I couldn't miss you, and you couldn't dodge."

Several breathless minutes passed with China not daring to take his eyes off the men in field-grey uniform. He had to keep flat on the top of the box-car for a crack marksman could pick him off at that range if he showed more than an inch or so of his head.

Then Sam Foster came crawling along the box-car tops to him.

"Thank goodness you didn't get off," Sam murmured, then ducked as from the end of the bridge came a sudden tat-tat-tat-tat, and bullets whined past him.

"You're growing careless," China reproved. "If you keep on like this you'll be getting hurt."

"Yes," Sam agreed, taking off his woollen cap-comforter and looking at the ragged ends of wool where a bullet had ripped through. "I felt the wind of that, just like a feather brushing across my head."

"Don't start getting poetic," China said rather sourly. "What have you come for, to tell me morning coffee is ready?"

"No." Sam scratched at the back of his head, then said

soberly, "We stopped 'cos Ted spotted a German army lorry at the other end of the bridge. They've got a machine gun mounted there, and men waiting for us."

"Holy mackerel," China whispered. "And what do we do now? Dive off the bridge? We can't back . . . there's two car-loads of Jerries at this end. Ted knows that."

"Well, for the first time since I've known him, Ted is giving us a choice," Sam said after a short pause. "He says if you like you can throw your tommy-gun away and surrender . . ."

"What!" China yelped.

"Or . . . you can come back to the engine, and take a chance with us," Sam went on. "Ted's going to blow up the bridge."

"Blow . . . b-b-b-blow up the bridge?" China spluttered. "Do you know what you are saying, Sam Foster? Blow up this bridge! And what happens to us? Has he forgotten we're on it? Sam," and he shook Sam by the arm. "Do you know what you are saying?"

Sam nodded unhappily.

"That's why he said: You can surrender if you want. He says we came here to blow up this bridge, and that's what he's going to do. Blow it up then try and drive off, past the Germans."

"Have a heart," China pleaded. "How can he? If he blows up the bridge, the whole flipping caboodle will go down into the gorge . . . box-cars, engine *and* us."

"Yes," Sam agreed. "I'm going back now. He's fixing the fuses for . . .!" Sam looking at his wrist-watch said: "I synchronised my watch with his, and he's aiming to blow the lot at eleven o'clock. If you decide to give yourself up . . . will you take this home for me?" and he held out a shabby wallet. "Give it my mum, if you get home safe."

China took the wallet. For the moment he was too dumbfounded to speak. Then Sam nodded, smiled, and slithering backwards to the forward end of the box-car, got over the gap and when he thought he was safe from the Germans, began to run towards the engine.

China lay on the box-car top for a minute or so before he finally stuffed Sam's wallet into an inside pocket. Then he pushed back his sleeve to look at his own watch. Sam had said Ted was going to blow the train up at eleven o'clock. A moment later China's eyes were bulging. It was no more than a minute and a half from eleven!

"The big yob," he snarled. "Why didn't he give me more time?" He fired a short burst at the Germans skulking about at the end of the bridge, then jumped to his feet and made a mad dash along the box-car tops in a desperate effort to reach the engine before eleven o'clock and the big bang.

When there were still three cars ahead of him he looked at his watch again. It was within seconds of eleven, and Sergeant Ted Harris had always been a stickler for punctuality.

"Wait for me, Ted," China yelled. "Ted . . . TED! Wait for me."

CHAPTER NINE

KAPUT—FINISH!

THE NEXT few seconds were the longest China Brown had ever known. Each second he expected to hear a tremendous boom, and feel the box-cars reeling from under him. When he finally came to the engine tender his leap was so wild that only a miracle kept him from sprawling over on to the track. Coal slithered under his feet. He reeled wildly, seemed about to topple off the tender, then gave a wild, mighty leap which could have been disastrous if Ted and Sam had not acted as buffers and prevented him from crashing headlong into the firebox door. They helped him from his knees, Ted saying:

"You *are* in a hurry, China. It isn't pay day, you know."

China, gasping for breath, drew in a deep breath, gave Ted a withering look then glancing at his wrist-watch said:

"Knowing how cuckoo you are for promptness I didn't have much time to get here. Sam said you were fixing zero hour for eleven . . . look at the time."

Ted looked at China's watch. It was now two minutes past eleven. Then he held out his own wrist, Sam did the same. Their watches showed the time to be two minutes to eleven. China's watch was four minutes fast!

108

"Well, I'm here," he said sheepishly. "What are we doing? Where's the driver and fireman?"

"I sent them off the bridge," Ted explained. "I told them I didn't want them to risk their necks when the big bang came."

"Well, what's he doing here?" China asked, pointing to a rather pale-faced Mike.

"Wouldn't go," Ted said laconically. "Reckoned he'd rather die with us than fall into the hands of the Germans. He could be wise at that. Anyway, you'd better shake hands, say your prayers, and then grab something. When I cross these two wires . . . things are going to happen. I've fixed the charges three coaches back . . . and if our engineers were telling the truth there'll be some *wump* when the stuff explodes."

China put his watch back four minutes, and with a grin explained:

"When we get to Heaven—if we go up, I don't want to be rushing out on parade there before the time. So long, Ted, Sam . . . Mike. Been nice knowing you, Mike." They all shook hands, then Ted looked at the second hand of his watch. Fifteen seconds to go.

"Everybody down," Ted ordered, and stepping over to the whistle lever he jerked it down to send a strident "Cock-a-doodle-doo" bellow into the quiet air. Then, he opened the regulator with one swift movement before dropping to his knees.

In the past few minutes the steam pressure had built up until a thin wisp was hissing from the safety valve. The pressure gauge showed two hundred pounds of steam. When Ted opened the regulator so quickly, it was against all the rules of good engine-driving. The result was a terrifying chuff-uff-uff-uff-uff as the seven-foot driving wheels spun dizzily, throwing off sparks but unable to get a grip.

Then Ted crossed the two bared ends of the wires. The army engineers in Italy had included everything in the demolition kit, even to a small battery, sufficiently powerful to explode the demolition charges. When Ted crossed the two bared wires he completed an electrical circuit.

Boom!

Several things happened at once, coinciding with the terrific roar and the sudden, eye-dazzling flash of far-reaching flame. What Ted had not confided to either Sam or China, was that he had uncoupled the engine and two of the box-cars from the rest of the train. He had also put a charge of explosives between the second and third box-cars, and had laboriously screwed up the brakes on the third box-car.

The major explosion occurred beneath the third box-car, which was standing over the middle of one of the long brick spans of the bridge. To the watching Germans on either bank the bottom seemed to drop out of that span and at the same moment the box-car above it jumped into the air, trying to pull up with it the other box-cars behind.

The second and first box-cars, along with the tender and engine, standing so motionless a moment before, suddenly leaped forward. Only a man faced with death or a prisoner-of-war cage would have taken such a risk; but Ted Harris had been taking risks for over four years, and though many of them had seemed crazy, they had all paid off.

While its driving wheels were spinning, and unable to get a grip on the rails, the massive locomotive literally got a "kick in the pants" from the explosion. The shock sent it lurching forward and at once the spinning driving wheels gripped. With a tremendous lurch the engine, tender and the two box-cars still coupled up, roared towards the safety of solid land.

Behind them there was terrifying chaos. The long brick viaduct was very old, and since the beginning of the war there had been no maintenance work done on it at all. The brickwork needed pointing, and in any case the bricks were beginning to crumble from old age.

The shattering thump from the explosive charges, followed by the shock as the big box-car which had been thrown into the air, fell over the side of the viaduct and began to drag the remainder of the box-cars after it, proved too much for a piece of building which was already unsafe.

For a second or so one of the tall archways swayed sideways. A gap appeared in the pillar some thirty feet down. Bricks flew out, some of them ground to yellow-red powder under the tremendous strain. Then, with box-cars falling off the viaduct the middle spans collapsed.

With a thunderous roaring and rumbling, hundreds of tons of brickwork began to disintegrate. In a growing cloud of dust they plunged a hundred and fifty feet down to the bed of the river, and with them went all but three of the long train of box-cars. These three remained on the bridge near the far bank simply because the coupling which attached them to the rest of

the train broke with a "twang" which went unheard
in the medley of sounds filling the air.

For the watching Germans it must have been a nerve-
shattering few seconds, and most of them instinctively
began to run away from the region of the bridge. Only
the odd man, here and there, remained calm enough to
realise that one part of the long train, the engine, tender and two coaches, were thundering on to safety.

In the cab of the big engine the few moments between the crash of the first explosion, and the sudden
lurch forward had been heart-shaking. The three
Britishers and young Mike were crouched down,
gripping whatever lay handy. They knew that if Ted
had made a mistake, they would plunge to their death
in the ravine.

Once they were moving, however, Ted Harris came
to life. He knew they were not out of danger, for they
had to pass the forty or more Germans who had been
calmly waiting for them to surrender. Ted had two
grenades ready. He whipped the safety pins out, and as
the engine rumbled on to solid ground again he
tossed a grenade on the right side, then one on the
left. As soon as he did that he dropped flat on the
throbbing footplate.

Whump . . . whump! The bursting of the grenades
sounded no more than thin whip cracks amid the
bellowing of the dying bridge; but they did give the
runaway a few seconds more grace. One or two of the
cooler-headed Germans had been raising automatic
rifles as the train drew nearer. The bursting grenades
sent them diving for safety, or collapsing as sizzling
shrapnel took its toll.

"Keep down . . . keep down!" Ted yelled as China Brown lifted his head. "We're not out of the wood yet. If they . . ."

"Crash . . . bang . . . bang . . . bang!"

At least one German had had the presence of mind to get down, and keep his Schmeisser handy. Now he poured burst after short burst at the engine cab. The bullets battered in a frightening drum beat against the steelwork of the cab, the flattened slips of lead shooting off in a volley of sparks.

Then, when it seemed they must be safe, there came a final short burst. There was no more than four shots, which emptied the Schmeisser magazine; but one bullet was enough to change the situation. It struck the plate-glass tube of the pressure gauge.

There was a fiendish howl. Splintered plate glass flew in all directions, and a moment later scalding steam and water enveloped the cab. The gauge glass was connected to the boiler at top and bottom. At the top, high-pressure steam came in, at the bottom, water; so that the driver could see just how much water there was in his boiler.

An experienced engine-driver could have remedied the damage in a matter of minutes. With a jacket over his head to protect his face from water and steam, he could have reached up to the brass cocks and shut off both water and steam. None of the Britishers were experienced locomotive-drivers. They knew how to stop, start and reverse an engine; but none of them had yet been called upon to deal with a broken pressure-gauge glass.

"Blimey, we're going to be cooked alive!" China

Brown yelled, inching his way up on to the coal in the tender. "What do we do now?"

Ted, Sam and Mike joined him on top of the coal. Here they were still almost hidden by steam, but in the cool air it had already lost its scalding heat, and was only wetting them.

Ted Harris wiped a dirty hand across his lips. It was not often he had to admit defeat, but for the moment he did not know what they could do. The engine, with only a coal tender and two box-cars to pull, was getting up quite a speed, for the regulator handle was on its last notch, giving the cylinders all the steam they could take.

What was more, the next four miles, into the seaside resort of Cavtat, was down a slight gradient. Every moment which passed saw them picking up more and more speed.

"Where does the railway run from Cavtat?" Ted yelled, laying a hand on the shoulder of the terrified Mike. "Shall we just run through the town?"

Mike stared at him for a moment, gulped, then shook his head.

"No. The railway ends in the station," he said jerkily. "We shall run into the station . . . and there the lines come to a stop."

"Strike a light," China howled. "Ted, we've got to do something. We're going to run slap into buffers, or something . . . and we must be doing ninety miles an hour."

"Don't be a fool, China," Ted snapped. "Forty . . . and no more."

"Well, forty miles an hour . . . that's plenty," China

yelled angrily. "We'll look like mincemeat if we're on this thing when it hits the buffers."

"Let's get on to the box-cars," Sam suggested. "There are brakes on them . . . we might be able to stop it that way."

They scrambled across the coal in the swaying tender, and now, no matter what Ted Harris insisted, there was no doubt they were doing over forty miles an hour. Steam and water was still blowing from the smashed gauge pipes, but with the track on a gradient even a dropping steam pressure was having little effect.

Ted and China crawled on to the second box-car and began to turn the big brake wheel. Sam and Mike wrestled with the brake wheel on the box-car next to the engine. For a minute it seemed as if they might succeed. Then the cars began to jolt as their wheels locked. They threw up a myriad dancing sparks; but they threatened disaster in another way. If their locked wheels caused them to jump the track the pile-up would be even more disastrous.

Ted waved a hand, signifying that Sam should ease off the brakes. It was then that Sam Foster had an idea. As he spun the big brake wheel he was looking down between the box-car and the coal tender. He saw the coupling chain which linked the box-car to the tender slacken. They did not need pulling along now. Their own weight was sufficient, on this gradient, to keep them going.

To Mike he screamed:

"Tell Ted to take his brakes off completely, I'm going to try and uncouple!"

Mike stared at him. Despite the dirt on his face his skin went ashen at the thought of anyone climbing down between the swaying box-car and the equally wild-riding tender. A slip would mean a horrible death under the box-car wheels. As Sam eased himself down between tender and box-car Mike scuttled along the top of the box-car to where Ted and China were crouched by the brake wheel. Neither of the Britishers could think of a way out. To leap from the box-cars on to the track side while they were tearing along at this break-neck speed would mean either death or the most terrible of injuries.

Mike yelled the news and for a moment Ted closed his eyes as he pictured Sam doing acrobatics between box-car and engine tender. He half decided to go along and try to help, but decided against it. Whatever happened would happen within the next sixty seconds. They were already in the suburbs of Cavtat. On either side there were pleasant-looking houses in a variety of pastel shades, and everything looked very peaceful. There had been no fighting around Cavtat, and Allied bombers had not even begun to plaster the coast towns of Yugoslavia.

They were within three quarters of a mile of the water front, and everything seemed to be racing towards them. He could see the small boats dotted about the blue water of the tiny bay. There was an E-boat moored alongside a small jetty. If there had been beach umbrellas on the sands, and tiny figures splashing about in the water it would not have been incongruous. In the sunshine Cavtat looked like a pleasant little holiday resort.

Ted was grim-faced as he waited for a signal from Sam to tell him that he had achieved what seemed the impossible—the unhooking of the heavy chain links which held the first box-car to the engine tender.

Something else was brewing of which he did not know. The splutter of water from the broken gauge pipe had stopped. It meant that all the spare water in the boiler had been blown out. The pressure in the steam-chest would be building up higher and higher; and there was a limit to what the old engine's boiler could stand. The needle on the pressure gauge was now jammed hard against the stop . . . well past the red line which denoted danger.

"He'll have to be quick, Ted," China Brown yelled hoarsely. "Stone the crows, if we hit the buffers at this speed we'll knock the whole flippin' station into the sea. We must be doing fifty at least."

"More like seventy," Ted retorted. "I'll give him another five seconds, then I'm going to put the brake on and chance it. If we could break the coupling we'd be all right."

"And Sam?" China asked.

Ted shrugged. This was one time when, no matter what he thought or did, he could not help Sam. There was not time to get across the two box-cars to warn Sam. The station was coming towards them at frightening speed.

"Okay?" Ted yelled, and with China to help him, began to spin the big, rusted brake wheel.

Down between the box-car and the engine tender Sam Foster had been fighting a terrifying battle. With one hand, he was hanging on to the narrow iron brakeman's ladder while with the other he kept trying to lift the heavy coupling chain off its hook. The links would slacken for a second as the box-car tried to over-run the tender. Then as the buffers ground together the box-car would be slowed for an instant and the coupling chain would tighten again.

Sam was beginning to despair, and the cold fingers of panic were closing round his heart when his luck turned. He felt the tension go off the heavy chain, and he gave another mighty heave. This time he was lucky. The big link came off the coupling hook and the box-car was freed from the engine tender.

"The brakes," Sam screamed. "The brakes, Ted. Put the brakes on." But the terrific clamour which was going on, the clank and bang as the buffers met, the clackety-clack as the wheels rolled over rail joints, all conspired to produce so much sound that no human voice could hope to compete. Yet, within seconds, the gap between box-car and tender started to widen. It was at that moment Ted Harris had begun to put on the box-car brakes.

Sam almost lost his hold on the car as it began to jolt and lurch under the drag of the hastily applied brakes. In the next few seconds Sam ceased trying to climb up the narrow iron ladder which led to the top of the box-car. The railway track curved slightly here before heading into the small station. From his position, Sam could see the station, and he could see the mighty engine eating up the distance between it and half-a-dozen coaches standing in the station itself. One or two men on the platform suddenly began to run as they realised that the approaching engine was travelling far too quickly for it to be stopped in time to prevent a crash.

The box-cars ground to a stop a hundred and fifty yards from the station, and as Sam lowered himself stiffly to the ground the runaway engine tore into the first of the coaches. Sam instinctively dropped flat on the track, as he would have done if he had seen a bomb sail out of the sky and plunge into the ground.

A second later the quietness was shattered by a sound which might have been the collapsing of a five- or six-story building. Eighty tons of engine, travelling at more than a mile a minute, crunched through the first and second coaches as if they had been made of nothing more substantial than matchbox wood.

There was a bellowing shriek of smashing timbers and rending metal. The engine seemed to claw its way into the air over the shattered coaches, crushing them even more, then there was a sudden blossoming of white vapour. The boiler had burst.

For seconds everything was blotted out. The roof of the station suddenly lifted into the air; sheet glass, metal struts, lamp brackets, all going up as if some invisible string had them in charge.

Sam scrambled under the box-car, and looking quickly back was in time to see Ted Harris, China Brown, and young Mike doing the same. Even so low down, however, they felt the hot blast of a titanic amount of energy released from the overcharged boiler.

Strangely enough none of them remembered hearing the mighty *Woof* which went with the explosion. What they did remember was the terrific air blast which

plucked at them even as they hugged the cinders between the rails. The box-cars reeled under the blow,
and would have been driven backwards had not the
brakes been firmly locked on the wheels of the second
box-car.

For a minute or more after that, things came down
out of the air, some large, some small. They crashed
on the ground, they hammered a devil's tattoo on the
box-cars; scraps of metal, wood, pieces of plate glass,
even a large part of a railway porter's trolley. It was
like a strange artillery barrage, with none of the
"shells" exploding.

Finally an eerie silence fell over the scene.

"We'd better get out of here," Ted called, and tried
with a dirt-grimed hand to wipe the dust from his lips.
"Mike . . . where can we hide?"

They looked around. A few minutes earlier there
had been a neat little station with the usual siding
adjacent. There had been a few railway trucks, some
small office buildings, and one or two large storage
sheds. None of them looked the same. The small
buildings were leaning drunkenly away from the
direction of the blast. The windows in the storage
places had all gone.

"Better hide somewhere in the buildings," Mike
suggested. "There are sure to be men coming quickly
now . . . soldiers; German soldiers. This way," and
crawling from beneath the box-car he led the way at a
trot towards one of the bigger buildings.

They entered the building by a shattered window,
and from there a few minutes later were able to
watch the arrival of soldiers; and later still gangs of

Yugoslav men, obviously hurriedly conscripted to help with the work of clearing the wreckage from about the station.

Mike said he would go out into the town and contact the local Partisan leader. The engine-driver had given them the man's name and address, for he himself was a Partisan.

"I shall come back after it is dark," Mike assured them. "We will have made a plan then how to get you away . . . in a boat."

"Don't leave it any later than you can help," Ted suggested. "Don't forget, we have promised to rescue those children."

Mike turned and looked Ted straight in the eyes. He gave a little shrug and shook his head slowly before saying:

"I am Yugoslav Partisan, Mr. Sergeant Harris. You are a British soldier. Do *you* forget things like hungry children?"

"I asked for that," Ted agreed, clapping a friendly hand on Mike's shoulders. "Sorry. I ought to realise that you wouldn't let us down. Anyway, be careful. If you are caught . . . we might be in the soup."

"In the soup?" Mike queried, and Ted laughed as he explained:

"In trouble. You see . . . we should be waiting for you to come back, and we might wait too long."

"You will not wait too long," Mike assured him, and, waiting his chance, climbed out through one of the broken windows and made his way across the debris-littered siding tracks.

An hour later, two German officers came and examined the box-cars on which Ted and the others had ridden. They inspected the brakes on the second box-car and must have come to the conclusion that the Britishers, who had made off on the engine when the railway viaduct was wrecked, had escaped just before the locomotive smashed into the station. The Germans at once started to search the surrounding buildings.

Luckily for Ted, Sam and China, they had realised that something like this might happen and had already decided on a hiding place. When German soldiers opened up the big shed, the three Britishers were precariously perched in the steel rafters, hidden from below by sacking stretched from beam to beam. None of the searchers gave more than a passing glance upwards, and eventually the place was locked up again.

"They never look up," China said. "Same if you are hiding in a wood. Climb in a tree and nobody looks up."

"Don't start crowing too soon," Ted advised. "Sam . . . open one of your ration tins, I think it's about time we had a snack and a smoke."

They nibbled the vitamin-packed chocolate and crunched the hard biscuits. There was no doubt they gave plenty of strength, but they were not like a good beef steak or a steaming plate of sausage and mash.

"For two pins I'd risk going outside to draw some water," China said. "I'll bet nobody would take any notice. We could make a cuppa. We've got tea, sugar and tubed milk."

"If you take one step towards the window, my lad," Ted threatened, "I'll forget I'm a three-striped sergeant, and give you one across the ear that'll make you think you've fallen off a ten-story building. You sit down and forget your cuppa. This isn't the time."

"Won't take a chance, will he, Sam?" China said ruefully. "Cor, I could drink a pint of tea without letting it touch the sides of my mouth."

"It's because I don't take stupid chances that we are still alive," Ted growled. "Now pipe down before you make me get annoyed."

The time dragged slowly on. Gangs of demolition men worked unceasingly in an effort to clear the tangle of twisted metal-work and shattered coaches out of the station. Oxy-acetylene cutters winked and spat their metal-eating blue flames, and there were occasional metallic crashes as some of the wreckage was dragged clear; but when darkness came down and stopped work there was still a lot to do.

"Hope they don't put a night shift on," Ted muttered. "It'd make things pretty awkward for us."

Silence settled over the station. Darkness closed in like a canopy, and with not even a signal light to break the gloom the three Britishers sat and waited for young Mike to return. They took turns standing near one of the shattered windows to catch the first sound of anyone coming near.

Not until nine o'clock was there the least sound. Then, from near the back of the building came a whisper.

"Hallo . . . Mr. Sergeant Harris, are you still here?" It was young Mike. "Come down to this end, please, quickly."

Sam was doing watch-dog at one of the windows at

the other end of the building and he began to walk down towards Mike. Ted and China who had been resting also got to their feet and made towards the sound of the voice.

Then, without warning, the darkness had gone. From the outside someone had switched on all the lights. They blazed down, revealing, with pitiless brilliance, the three Britishers as they halted, each looking up instinctively towards the lights above them. A moment later men appeared at the shattered windows —Germans with Schmeisser automatics. There were at least a dozen of them, and the three hands which had begun to move swiftly towards pistol holsters, checked.

"You had better lift your hands above your heads," Mike called. "If you don't, the Germans will shoot you dead."

Ted lifted his hands, an action copied by Sam and China. There were times when resistance was impossible, and this was one of them.

CHAPTER TEN

THE HAPPY TRAITOR

A KEY RATTLED in the old-fashioned lock of the big door, and when the door swung open a German sergeant stepped briskly inside, followed by an officer. While the sergeant covered the three Britishers the men at the windows disappeared one after the other, and in two's marched into the store place.

Ted Harris watched young Mike climb through the broken window. The Britisher's face did not betray his feelings, and his voice sounded almost casual when he said:

"So you are a Yugoslav Partisan, are you, Mike? *You* don't forget hungry children. I suppose you were born a dirty little rat and you can't help being a dirty rat," and turning away he spat out.

For a moment there was silence. The Germans were frisking the three Britishers under the watchful eyes of the German sergeant and the officer. They took everything, putting them in a little pile on a piece of clean rag. Mike came round to face Ted and there was fury in his voice when he said:

"If it were not wrong to strike a prisoner of war, Mr. Sergeant Harris, I would show you that I am a rat with teeth. I am only small, but I am a fighter. I shall tell you something. The Germans have put notices up in the town offering a reward for you. I can use money just as much as anyone else. That is why I brought them here."

Ted turned away. He felt sick. Not sick because he had been taken prisoner. That was one of the things any commando had to risk. He felt sick to think that this youngster, whom in the past thirty-six hours he had grown to like, had deliberately sold them.

When the searching was completed the three Britishers were ordered to march to the door. A minute later a covered lorry arrived and, under the watchful eyes of the Germans, Ted, Sam and China climbed over the tailboard and into the lorry.

Six men got in with them. The officer climbed in with the driver. The back was fastened in place. The sergeant called his remaining six men to attention, and after the lorry moved off he began to march them back to their barracks.

In the back of the lorry Ted Harris quickly decided that to attempt to escape would be merely signing a death-warrant. Three of the men had big torches. These were held so that the beams shone on the canvas top of the lorry, and the reflected light lit up the inside of the lorry. The other three Germans sat with Mauser pistols at the ready. In the well-lit lorry it was quite impossible for anyone to make even the slightest move without it being seen. Moreover, the three Britishers were seated with their backs to the driving cab. To get out they would have to force their way past their six-man escort.

"Anybody got a cig?" China asked, looking hopefully round, and made a motion of smoking.

"Sorry, Britisher," one of the men holding a torch said quietly. "It is more than we dare do. Maybe when you are locked up someone will giff you a smoke."

"Hm, you speak good English," Ted murmured. "Have you lived in England?"

The man, a pudgy fifty-years-old at least, nodded and shrugged apologetically:

"I am twenty years in Birmingham. I like, very much. Maybe we meet again . . . when this verdammt war iss over."

"What are they going to do with us?" Ted asked.

The smile on the German's face vanished. He shook his head pessimistically, shot a quick glance at the other five, and apparently decided not to say anything.

The lorry rolled slowly out of the station yard, and because of a wrecked building had to make a detour through an area of wooden sheds, warehouses and shipping offices. They were stopped once by sentries who looked in the back of the lorry even as the vehicle began to move on again. It annoyed China, who growled disgustedly:

"Making a flippin' peepshow of us, that's what they are. It strikes me they've never seen any prisoners before. And if I . . . oops!"

The exclamation was jerked out of him as the lorry came to a sudden halt, and a moment later the officer in the cab was heard blistering the hide of the driver with a torrent of oaths. The engine was stopped, and it was almost as if they had run into a brick wall.

Ted tensed. He had that sudden crawling feeling at the back of his neck which came when something unexpected was going to happen. He spat on his hands, then wiped them on the front of his battledress blouse. It was a gesture which passed unnoticed by the guards, but to Sam and China it said plainly enough:

"If there's half a chance, lads, jump for it."

They heard the driver start his engine again, felt the slight jerk as he got into gear, then the lorry moved a mere four inches before stopping once more. Again with the curious sensation of having run into a wall. The engine died once more.

A shout from the officer brought two of the men with torches to their feet. The back of the lorry was dropped down and while the third man with the torch kept his beam shining full on the Britishers his two companions with torches dropped out on to the road. That they found something unexpected was obvious from a sudden shout which brought their officer and the lorry driver round at a run.

Almost at once there was a rush of feet. Not the clatter of hobnailed boots, not even the quieter sound of leather-soled shoes, but the soft, rather menacing pad-pad-pad of shoes and boots muffled by having rags wrapped about them. A stifled yell of alarm from one of the Germans was drowned by even stranger noises, a series of cracked-bell notes as heavy clubs came down on steel-helmeted heads.

The four Germans still in the lorry sprang to instant action; but were halted before any of them could get to the tailboard. Someone shone a brilliant light into the lorry, resting the torch on the lorry floor. In the light, silent and frightening, a hand appeared, a hand which held a grenade.

In the brilliant light it was not difficult to see that the safety pin had been taken out. The grenade was live! It was far deadlier than a pistol. A man with an automatic could fire one shot at a time, and there was always the chance that the bullet might miss its target. The man who held that grenade need only open his fingers wide to detonate the innocent-looking thing he held. If it exploded in the lorry it would scatter death and deadly wounds among British and German alike. Grenades can be fused for seven-second detonation, or fused for immediate detonation.

"It could be a one-second fuse," Ted snapped, looking across towards the pudgy German who understood English. "For pete's sake don't do anything."

"*Ja-ja*—" the German gasped, and babbled a quick explanation to his three companions. Blinded by the brightness of the light shining in on them, it was quite impossible to see who was behind the torch, or what was going on in the narrow road outside.

They could tell by the grunts and thuds that a fight was in progress. The Germans had been taken by surprise, but they were putting up a good fight. Ted, China and Sam were itching to get out and lend a hand; but there were three very good reasons why they sat taut and still. There were four Germans still in the lorry with them. The fat one who spoke English sat with an electric torch in his lap, the other three held Mauser pistols, and they were pointed at the prisoners.

"If we don't get out now we never will," China whispered urgently.

"You move when I say, and not before," Ted whispered back, equally urgently. He was trying to see through the glare of the light, but it was quite impossible. Out there in the darkness the fight seemed to be lessening in ferocity. There were thumps and gasps, occasional clanging noises suggesting a steel helmet rolling on the road. Then, quite suddenly, there was a new sound; the sharp crack of a pistol shot.

A man screamed, then came the clatter of feet as someone raced away into the night.

"That's a Jerry," Sam muttered. "The others sounded as if they were in their stockinged feet."

A man yelled something in Yugoslav. There came the softer pad-pad-pad of muffled feet, suggesting two or three men going in pursuit of the escaping German. Ted, China and Sam were almost dancing with impatience, waiting to be called out of the lorry before German reinforcements arrived. Yet the man holding the grenade on the edge of the tailboard never moved. His brilliant torch still lit up the inside of the lorry, his hand still remained clasping the release lever of the grenade.

Something was happening outside, yet no one spoke. Whoever they were, out there in the dark, they knew their business and orders were apparently not necessary. Then when the three Britishers were beginning to despair of anything happening, a man called into the lorry. He spoke German, and his order was obeyed without hesitation. One by one three Mauser pistols were tossed out into the darkness. Then the pudgy German leaned across to Ted and passed him his torch. As he did so he whispered:

"Partisans! I wish you luck. They are devils!" Then he was walking towards the tailboard and into the darkness. Still the unseen man with the grenade did not move. His torch flooded the lorry with light, he still held that devilish handful of death poised on the rim of the tailboard.

"What are they doing?" China asked irritably. "Somebody must have heard the shot. And at least one of the Jerries got away. They'll have the whole place round our ears in a few minutes, and our chance gone for . . ."

He stopped there for the grenade was suddenly removed, and a moment later young Mike scrambled into the lorry.

"It will soon be all right now," he said hurriedly. "We are going out to the jetty. You will be put aboard the German E-boat. I am sorry not to have been able to tell you how things would work out. I saw the leader of the Partisans, and he told me the German command was worried . . . they thought many more British were here. So we had to comfort them . . . make them realise there were only three. That is why I claimed the reward they were offering . . . and brought them to the railway yard."

"I see!" Ted did not sound enthusiastic. The youngster might be telling the truth, and indeed they had been rescued from the hands of the Germans, but what was going to follow he did not know, and he felt uneasy.

Mike realised from Ted's voice that the Britisher doubted him and he shrugged.

"It is no use me trying to explain," he said. "Maybe actions speak better, eh? We move off in a minute. Then you see how clever we Partisans are."

He had hardly said that when men began to clamber into the lorry, and the three Britishers just stared. They were Germans! They wore the typical coal scuttle steel helmets, the German uniform jacket, with normal regimental flashes on the tunic collar. The one great difference was that they were all grinning triumphantly.

The back of the lorry was slammed up, the engine roared to life, and as they moved off the night sky suddenly ceased to be deep blue-black, for a star-shell burst high in the air, flooding the whole area with a vivid incandescent brilliance.

"That's it," Ted growled, and nodded his thanks as one of the "Germans" handed him a Schmeisser and two spare magazines. "The bloke who got away has raised the alarm. If our driver doesn't get his foot down we've had it."

Yet the driver did not accelerate. He drove along at no more than about fifteen miles an hour, and even above the rumble of the engine, and the usual noises made by a lorry going over cobbles, they heard the thin wail of a siren. The Germans were really wakening up to the fact that one of their lorries had been ambushed.

"Ah-ha," Sam murmured a few moments later. "Water."

Several of the uniformed men also pointed to the water, easy enough to see for several starshells were now in the air, and the smooth surface of the water reflected the light in dazzling fashion.

Through the back of the lorry the three Britishers could see they were being taken along a jetty, at which both Sam and China suggested by signs that they too, could usefully use a weapon. They got headshakes as answers. None of their "captors" had any spare arms.

Then the lorry ground to a stop. A man gave an order in German, and the tailboard of the lorry was dropped by someone who had been riding in the lorry cab. The "Germans" got out and standing stiffly to attention waited while Ted, Sam and China descended.

The scene which met their eyes could have been beautiful, had the danger not been so great. Star-shells were being fired at intervals into the air, so that the whole of the harbour area, and the waterfront of Cavtat was brilliantly lit up. Tiny boats rocked gently at anchor, and a few yards away the long, sinister-looking shape of the German E-boat lay black against the quay wall.

That she had been warned to put out to sea, or perhaps only into the harbour where she would be safe from boarding, was obvious. Men were busy unlooping the mooring lines and there was a purr from her powerful diesels.

There was a shout, in German, from someone who had just got out of the lorry. It was the German officer who had first captured the three Britishers. Now he was obeying the orders of a man who was pressing a Mauser pistol against his ribs.

"You are to take three British prisoners aboard, Lieutenant," the German yelled, and was answered angrily by someone in the E-boat's wheel-house who demanded the authority for such a thing. He called to the quay that he had just received orders to take his vessel into the bay in case of a surprise attack.

"Not without these three Britishers," he was told. "Stand by to take them aboard."

Then the E-boat commander made a mistake. He left the wheel-house, dropped down two steps and came to the side of his vessel protesting angrily. Then the group of men who had been standing on the far side of the lorry, erupted into action. They swept across the few yards which separated them from the edge of the quay, and within seconds there was a free-for-all going on aboard the E-boat.

Men stormed up from below, and there was a great mêlée in progress when from the shore end of the quay came a piercing whistle, and as the three Britishers turned to look in that direction they saw the headlights of at least two vehicles moving towards them.

"Get aboard, lads, and give our pals a hand," Ted ordered. Then, kneeling, he cocked the Schmeisser, pushed off the safety catch, and sent a short, exploratory burst along the quay.

He was testing the gun for firing, and when he saw the sparks on the cobbles which told him he was firing low, he lifted his sights a little, fired another burst and had the satisfaction of seeing one headlamp in the first vehicle go out.

He fired again, and the second headlamp went out, but this time he knew it had been switched off. He could tell that by the sudden fade. Not an immediate black-out as happens when the bulb has been smashed.

For a few moments the lights of the second vehicle remained on, revealing the first one in silhouette, and Ted's lips went to a thinner line as he saw the dark figures of men spreading out across the quay. A few moments later bullets began to whine above him, some of them began slapping into the hull and the upper works of the E-boat.

Ted rattled off another short burst from the Schmeisser, and then he heard young Mike calling him.

"Mr. Sergeant Harris . . . come aboard. You must come aboard, at once."

Ted had three yards of quay to cross before he could drop down on to the deck of the E-boat, and tough, battle-hardened warrior though he was, he hesitated. There was an absolute barrage of shots whining along the quay now. The Germans down there were hotting up the battle.

Ted emptied his Schmeisser, then rolled over and over until he was on the very brink of the quay. A moment later he dropped down on to the deck. The battle was ending. Stretched out all around were unconscious Germans, and a few Partisans who had also been knocked out.

Mike found Ted and yelled:

"Can you take her out to sea, Mr. Sergeant Harris? Sam is in the engine-room with a German. You must do it now. The Germans are bringing reinforcements up." And he pointed down the quay where twin lights denoted the approach of more vehicles.

"To sea!" Ted paused for an instant, then nodded. It was the only way out, and though he had handled smaller boats than this, he was not so sure he could take an E-boat away from the quay without ripping off her screws along the quay wall, or doing some other equally crippling damage.

When he got into the wheel-house there was a con-

stant "thump-thump-thump" going on all around as
Germans on the quay, now no more than a hundred
yards distant blazed away.

There was a speaking tube in the wheel-house and
taking a chance that it connected with the engine-
room, Ted called down it:

"Give me half speed ahead."

To his delight Sam Foster's voice came eerily back
to him with a chuckled:

"Aye-aye-sir."

A few seconds later the ship began to throb under
the drive of the powerful engines. The E-boat began to
move and then, just as the German lorry had done less
than twenty minutes earlier, the vessel came to an
abrupt stop.

Ted swore. He had no idea what had happened, and
when he popped his head out of the starboard window
of the wheel-house he was all too conscious of the
vicious flashes on the quay, drawing nearer and nearer.
The firing from the E-boat was thinning out now, for
the Partisans were running out of ammunition.

Then, above the pandemonium came a yell from
young Mike.

"Stop the engine, Mr. Sergeant Harris. The mooring lines are still on."

"Stop engines," Ted called down the speaking tube,
and a few moments later the throbbing grew less
pronounced as the screws were thrown out of gear.
The E-boat drifted back to the quayside, slackening the
mooring lines.

Young Mike sprang ashore, unlooped the stern mooring line, an action which at once allowed the stern to

begin moving away from the quay. Then he raced along to the bow mooring line. He tugged for a moment at the taut line, then whipping out his knife began to saw at it.

By this time the E-boat was trying to get away from the quay as her stern edged farther and farther from the moss-covered stone wall. The tautness of the mooring line helped Mike and by the time he had sawed half way through the hawser, the remaining strands began to snap under the strain.

It was at this crucial moment that the driver of the second German vehicle moved to one side and switched on his headlamps. Two powerful beams of light lit up the quay from end to end, revealing the boy at work on the mooring line.

Tat-tat-tat-tat-tat. There was an absolute crescendo of shots as half a dozen men opened up with automatics; but Mike had dropped flat. As he did so the weakened mooring line parted with a resounding *twang* and the E-boat was free. She reeled a little, and Ted Harris, wondering how long he could stand in the small wheel-house and remain uninjured, promptly called down to Sam in the engine room for half speed ahead.

The E-boat vibrated and began to move. Ted swung the wheel hard over and the long slim vessel, a great boil of foam churning at her stern, began to turn hard to port.

It was then, as she began to gather speed that he chanced a look through the starboard window. He got a quick impression of the quay, brightly lit, of German soldiers advancing from behind the shelter of their

trucks and small tracked vehicles—and of a boy racing
like the wind for the far end of the jetty, dodging
wildly from side to side as Schmeissers began another
chant of death.

During the next few seconds, Ted Harris, who always
prided himself on keeping his mind on the job in hand,
completely forgot that he was at the wheel of a powerful, fast moving German E-boat, with almost a score
of Yugoslav partisans aboard, as well as his two men,
Sam and China.

Mouth half open he was silently urging Mike on,
silently cursing the German gunners, and wincing
each time a tracer bullet with its glowing end showing
where it was going, moved like a firefly past the boy.

Then Mike went down, and stayed down.

CHAPTER ELEVEN

ALL—OR NOTHING

THERE WAS an urgent yell from the after deck of the
E-boat, a warning to Ted that he should straighten up
his rudder or they would turn a complete circle and
head back towards the quay they had just left. The
powerful engines were only opened up at half throttle,
but since an E-boat can do close to forty knots—close
on 48 miles an hour—they were moving at a very fast
speed indeed.

Ted reached for the voice tube and yelled down:

"Shut off, Sam." Then turning to the window he
bawled: "China . . . CHINA BROWN!"

"Yep!" The voice came from just outside the wheel-
house, but not at deck level. A moment later China
was leaning from the roof of the wheel-house, looking
in at Ted from an upside down position.

"What the . . . what are you doing up there, you
fool?" Ted raved. "Look . . . Mike's down on the quay.
He may be dead. He may only be wounded; but we're
going in for him."

"I thought you might," China yelled back. "That's
why I'm up here. There's a quick-firer mounted on
your roof. Gimme a minute and I'll do something."

Ted turned to the wheel again, spun it, and steadied
the E-boat on a course which could take her slap into
the quay. He stared through the windows ahead,

seeing the small figures of Germans hurrying along the quay. They were brilliantly lit by the glare of the headlamps. He thought, but could not be sure, that he could see the figure of young Mike, slumped face down on the cobbles.

Then without warning, the little wheel-house seemed to jump solidly as from above the quick-firer went into action:

Whump . . . whump . . . whump . . . whump!

Each *whump* was a shot fired, and the kick of the gun sent a quiver through everything. Ted could feel the jar of it from the soles of his feet to the top of his head. From where he stood he saw the immediate result. There was a sudden flash of fire against the quay wall. A second or so later another round exploded, a little higher, and in the flash it was possible to see fragments of stone or cement flying through the air.

The third Bofors-type shell struck something on the opposite side of the quay and a small brick building erupted into a jumble of shattered brickwork and clouds of dust.

In the light from the headlamps the advancing Germans were hesitating. The next shell made them turn tail. They ran for shelter, and at that moment the men still clustered about the German vehicles opened up with everything they had at the E-boat. Bullets hammered at the light armour plating on the wheel-house front. They sent long jagged sparks tearing off into the night. They ricochetted everywhere, and the Yugoslav Partisans did the wisest thing possible: dived below for shelter.

Then China turned his gun towards the German trucks and cars. Bullets from that group were droning everywhere until the first shell went home. It struck a car fair and square, and within thirty seconds the quay was lit in a ruddy glare as a burst petrol tank went up in flames.

Ted spun his wheel desperately as he realised they were in imminent danger of hitting the quay wall in a head-on collision. He yelled down the voice-tube for "full speed astern" and the vibrations which followed when his order was obeyed drew a yowl of protest from China who was having difficulty in sighting his gun.

"Stop . . . stop . . . STOP!" Ted roared, glaring at the speaking tube as if it were responsible for the fact that they were now beginning to go backwards, away from the quay wall.

Whump . . . whump . . . whump . . .! The gun on the wheel-house top restarted its slow, methodical hammering, the shells turning the clutter of trucks into a chaos of burning, shattered vehicles. Then, suddenly, the comforting whump-whump stopped.

Ted swore. He had a feeling that China had bought one. Protected though he was by a thin armoured shield, the Britisher was not proof against the odd ricochetting bullet which might find its way through the joints in the shield.

"Sam!" Ted bellowed at the voice tube again. "Gimme slow ahead, then come up on deck. I need you."

He waited until the E-boat began to move gently forward and away. He spun the wheel to edge them broadside on to the quay, then with a last yell to Sam to stop everything, he bounced out of the wheel-house and scrambled up the short ladder which led to the wheel-house top.

China Brown was on his knees, a trickle of blood on his chin. He was coughing desperately and for a moment Ted's heart went cold. A bullet through the lungs. That was what it sounded like.

"Hang on a few minutes, China," he pleaded. "I'll see to you when I've got that load of tripe out of the way."

He straddled China so that he could get at the gun sights, and with a hand on the gun trip took steady aim. The Germans may have been temporarily demoralised by the sudden change of fortune, but they were now beginning to hit back again. From behind their blazing trucks and cars some of them were starting to pour a withering fire into the E-boat, and they were doing so at a range of no more than a hundred and fifty yards.

Whump . . . whump . . . whump . . . whump . . .

Shell after shell smashed into the blazing trucks. Metal flew everywhere. More petrol tanks were burst and added their flames to the already roaring fire. Then Sam Foster came on deck, pushing before him at the point of a gun the terrified German engineer.

A Yugoslav Partisan took over the engineer and Sam yelled up to Ted to ask what he wanted.

"On the quay," Ted bellowed. "Look for Mike. He's been hit. Bring him aboard . . . even if he's dead, bring him aboard."

Whump . . . whump . . . whump . . . and then the

gun stopped. It had not jammed. It was simply that
the finest gun in the world is no use without ammunition, and the sickle-shaped feeding tray was now
empty. Ted stood and swore. Young Sam Foster was
now up on the quay, and bending down to pick up
Mike.

The Germans were momentarily under cover, afraid
to come out in case the gun on the E-boat began blast-
ing at them again. If the silence continued for another
twenty or thirty seconds, they would guess what had
happened, and that would be the end. They were not
short of small arms ammunition, and without the
threat of shelling, could come out and literally plaster
the E-boat from end to end with automatic fire.

In the silence Ted could hear the roaring of the flames
licking twenty and more feet high from the blazing
wreckage of the trucks. He thought he saw movement
beyond them. Men getting to their feet and peering
past the burning vehicles to see what was happening.

Forgetting that China was injured Ted bent down
and grabbing his comrade by the arm he shook him
and yelled:

"Is there no other ammunition?"

There was a splutter of disgust and irritation, then
China heaved himself unsteadily to his feet. He wiped
the blood from his chin with the back of his hand then
turned and lurched to a stack of boxes.

A single rifle spat fire from beyond the burning
wreckage and a bullet smacked into the gunshield.
China Brown dragged a box towards his gun and kicked
open the lid. Banging at his chest for a moment with
the end of his right hand forefinger he croaked:

"Got a side-swiping ricochet in the mouth. Look . . . knocked a flippin' tooth down my throat. Can feel it here," he banged at his chest then began to load shells into the feed arm and Ted restarted firing.

From the direction of the quarter mile distant beach there was a flicker of fire, and an anti-tank shell screamed overhead. Ted yelled to Sam to hurry. There was no need for any yelling now. Some of the Yugoslav Partisans had come on deck, and with reckless bravery had scrambled up on to the quay to give Sam a hand. Within seconds they made their breathless return to the boat, carrying the limp body of Mike.

Ted fired three last rounds into the flaming wreckage then, abandoning the gun, he scrambled back into the wheel-house and bellowed for half speed ahead. He was sweating with anxiety. The men behind that anti-tank gun on the beach knew their job. They had dropped shells beyond the E-boat, dropped them short, dropped them on the right and on the left, and any moment they would drop one right in the middle of that area. If they did, and if they were lucky enough to hit either the engine room or the fuel tanks, that would be the finish.

When there was no immediate response to his command for half speed astern Ted yelled into the voice tube again, and gripped it so tightly that the thin aluminium bent under his strength.

"Full speed ahead!" he bellowed. "Sam . . . FULL SPEED AHEAD!"

Crash!

The E-boat seemed to sink down a foot then leap into

the air. The anti-tank gunners had been just a little too slick, and had got in their final, well-aimed shell a few moments before Sam Foster could get his nerve-shattered German engineer back at the controls.

There was a roar, the shriek of twisted metal, the whine as pieces of steel crashed against more solid metal-work and ricochetted off into the night. Then there was more light. The E-boat feeding quarters in the midships were on fire.

A few moments later the decks began to quiver as the engines came to life. Down below, though he knew something unexpected had happened, Sam Foster was standing by the side of the German engineer, a pistol in his right hand. He asked for full speed and he got it.

With the tremendous power of her triple screws lifting her bows, the E-boat went across the water for the first thirty seconds in an odd, skittering rush. Then she seemed to shake herself and settled back into a steadily increasing rush of speed. The tremendous flow of air over her fanned the fire in the midships, and it was impossible for anyone to do anything about it. With the E-boat roaring along at such a speed any man who was foolish enough to have dipped a bucket over the side would either have had his arm wrenched off, or would have been plucked over the side to drown in the darkness of the night.

Nor did Ted dare stop. The anti-tank gunners were still firing at him, and the glow from the burning midships helped them keep somewhere near the target. Though no one saw them, shells plopped into the sea at regular intervals, and some of them were within thirty yards of the vessel.

At the end of ten minutes Ted was forced to stop. In the little control room Sam Foster was trying to keep a German engineer at his post, when the man seemed to be on the verge of becoming a gibbering maniac. He kept pointing to a dial and shrieking at Sam.

Sam Foster watched the needle on the dial swing steadily round the face until it reached a point where the card was shaded red. At this part the word *Achtung!* was painted on the glass. The engineer, the sweat of fear rolling down his face, jabbed at Sam's chest, jabbed at the dial, then gesticulated to show that any moment now the ship would blow up.

Sam took a chance and ordered the man to shut down the engines.

Up above the flames leapt skywards when the speed dropped to no more than a crawl, and from then on everything that would hold water was used to dip into the sea and pour gallon after gallon on the flames. The acrid stench which salt water on burning wood produces was beyond description.

In the wheel-house Ted Harris was busy doing a spot of first-aid work on China Brown. He had been struck a glancing blow on the teeth, either by a ricochetting bullet, or a small fragment of flying metal. It had knocked out one of his front teeth, and cut his lip badly.

"I always said you opened your mouth too often, China," Ted murmured as he dabbed at the cut lip. "If you kept your trap shut like old Sam Foster does, this might not have happened. It should be a lesson to you for the . . . future." The last word came out slowly, for the wheel-house had suddenly become almost as light as day.

Ted turned to stare seawards and the grin faded. He could not see the vessel behind that searchlight, but there was no doubt it was a vessel. The light swung off the burning E-boat, then back again, as if the officer in command of the unseen ship was searching the area in case there was any other vessel in the offing. They had got six miles out to sea, only to be caught. It was the worst possible luck.

"Well, they tell me the Jerry surgeons are very good, China old scout," Ted said sadly, handing his friend the blood-stained First Field Dressing with which he had been trying to staunch the bleeding. "It looks as if our luck has run out."

They both came out of the wheel-house. On deck the men were still fighting the fire furiously, and beginning to get the better of it. In the stress of the moment no one seemed to have noticed that a searchlight was playing on them.

Then the light was switched off, and five minutes later there came a stentorian bellow, obviously over a ship's loud hailer. Ted shrugged. It was in German. He knew that *Ja* meant yes, and *Nein* meant no; apart from that his knowledge of German was nil.

The shout rolled across the water again. It was a threat that if any action was taken the boat would be blown out of the water. Then the searchlight came on again and a minute or so later a boat came bobbing over the water, four men pulling at the oars, and a further five seated in the stern, all armed.

"Keep on with the buckets, lads," Ted bellowed when some of the Yugoslav Partisans stopped to watch the approaching boat. "Maybe he thinks we're smugglers, or something."

He dipped a hand over the side and scooping up some salt water wiped it over his face. He felt coated with dirt, and he pulled a wry face as he felt the stubble of three days, growth of beard on his chin. Looking across to the approaching boat he yelled:

"Okay, this way, I'm in command."

At once someone in the boat gave an order and the oars were lifted out of the water. A torch was switched on and focused on Ted. Then a clear-cut, incisive voice demanded:

"Who the devil are you?"

For a moment Ted could not believe his ears. Even China, mopping his sore lip croaked in astonishment, then he nudged Ted in the back and with unbelief in his voice muttered:

"It's the Navy . . . its the flippin' British Navy."

Ted swallowed. He almost felt like pinching himself to make sure this was not one of those lovely dreams which fade away the moment a man wakens up. Then he yelled back:

"Sergeant Harris, sir . . ." and after a momentary hesitation during which he decided not to say which army unit he belonged to, added: "British army."

The boat was rowed alongside, and a very smart and efficient-looking Naval officer came aboard, followed by four grim-looking armed sailors.

"We saw the fireworks ashore, and then your fire.

What's been going on? Have you got your pay book,
or identity papers?"

"No pay book, nothing, sir," Ted apologised. "We
have been in the hands of the Germans. They stripped
us. But I have two more men with me who can cor-
roborate my story. And there's a bunch of Yugoslav
Partisans here who'll bear out what I have to say."

The naval lieutenant looked round for a moment
then ordered Ted into the boat. He left five armed men
on the E-boat, and as the fire was now dying down to no
more than a fading glow, told the "Snotty" to make
sure no lights were shown and all men were kept on
the seaward side of the vessel to ensure no signalling to
the distant shore.

Aboard the destroyer, for that was what the vessel
was, were men of Ted's own unit. The destruction of
the railway viaduct outside Cavtat was reckoned so
important that the failure of the first landing party
had called for swifter measures, and a landing party
was to be put ashore to wreck the viaduct without the
help of the Yugoslav Partisans.

Some of the commandos recognised Ted immediately,
and when he insisted that the viaduct had been destroyed, several Yugoslav Partisans were brought
over from the smouldering E-boat to be questioned
individually, only then did the commander of the
destroyer decide Ted was telling the truth.

"Good show, Sergeant," he said finally. "Sorry, we
can't waste time towing that E-boat across the Adriatic.
So we'll put some explosives aboard, sink her, and
with a little luck you'll be back in Bari within twelve
hours."

"What about the children, sir . . . and Curly Bates?"

"The children?"

"Oh, yes, I forgot I hadn't told you that," Ted apologised, and went on to tell how they had gone into the mountains with Mike to take food to the starving children and how he had left Curly Bates with them.

"I told Curly, and the youngsters, that we'd be back within three or four days to take them off, and get them over to Italy, sir. They're in a shocking state. Need a lot of feeding up, and doctoring, too."

The destroyer commander shook his head slowly.

"I'm sorry, Sergeant. You know this is war. War on a massive scale. If I could help the children, I would. But I have definite orders to return to Italy the moment the commandos returned to report that the viaduct was destroyed. I just could not take off your children. Terribly sorry, Sergeant. I mean that, too."

"Yessir," Ted clicked his heels and drew himself to attention. "Could I ask a favour, sir?"

"You can ask, but I don't know whether I can grant it," was the quiet reply. "Go ahead and ask."

"I have just remembered, sir," Ted said tonelessly, "that I left some quite valuable equipment ashore. Special radio kits and so on. May I have permission to go ashore to pick this stuff up."

"What? Are you serious?"

"Yessir." Ted's face was quite expressionless. "I think that E-boat will keep afloat. I could get inshore at dawn, farther down the coast and pick up the stuff . . ."

"I'm sorry, I couldn't wait," was the firm reply. "If Jerry knew there was a British destroyer in these waters we'd have dive bombers and E-boats buzzing round like bees round a jam pot. No, I'm afraid . . ."

"Beg pardon for interrupting, sir," Ted cut in. "I wasn't thinking of you staying here. I think we could go in, get our stuff . . . and perhaps sail the E-boat across to Bari . . . you know, take it quiet-like."

"And what about the children you spoke of?"

"Oh, well," Ted coughed, and the corners of his mouth twitched as he tried to control a grin. "If I could find room for one or two of them . . . maybe I'd take a chance and see if I could get them across."

"Why didn't you join the Navy?" the officer suddenly asked, and allowed himself a momentary grin. "We could have used you in the Silent Service. All right, Sergeant Harris. I have no jurisdiction over you. I thought I was capturing a vessel under enemy command. I see it is being used by the British Army, and I have no wish to interfere."

"You mean I can do it, sir?" Ted's face lit up.

"I'll leave you here for a few minutes," was the quiet reply. "If you write down what you think you need— in the way of arms, I will see if I can supply you. If there is any other way I can help, I will. We don't normally do this, Sergeant," and he thrust out his right hand. "The best of luck . . . and if you do get back to Bari . . . ask for me at the Naval Officers' club. When I am in mufti I'll be delighted to stand you the longest drink of your life." He clapped a hand on Ted's arm then left the room while Ted sat down to jot down some of the things he thought he would need from the destroyer's armoury.

An hour later the destroyer slid quietly out to sea, heading south-west for Bari, Italy. Stores had been transferred from her to the E-boat. Her engine-room artificers had been to check the E-boat's engines and fuel supply. They were satisfied that she could get across the Adriatic to Italy under her own power.

Aboard the destroyer were Mike, who had a bullet through his shoulder, but was in no danger of dying, and several of the Partisans who were wounded and needed the skilled attention of a doctor.

Left behind were a group of unwashed, unshaven men. Three of them were in ragged commando rig. One of the Partisans who had been a fisherman took the wheel of the E-boat, and just before day broke, nosed her into the beach almost at the identical spot where the old schooner had put Ted and his three pals ashore some days earlier.

Everything was quiet for an hour, then a small boy sauntered down towards the beach. He was one of the refugee children, and he led Ted Harris and some of the Partisans up the hill to the cave where Dravadavitch and his men had ambushed the Fighting Four earlier in the week. Curly Bates and the children were there, waiting. There were scenes of wild rejoicings when it was known that, though accommodation would be crowded, Ted proposed to try to get all the children aboard the E-boat.

When Ted asked about Dravadavitch and his men

Curly Bates raised his eyebrows, scratched pensively behind one ear for a moment, then grinned.

"We kinda left them back there in the hills," he confessed. "Mind you, we didn't leave them to starve. Oh, no. I couldn't do that. I left them with a pound tin of bully for each two men . . . and in exchange I carted off the left boot of each of 'em. I told 'em where they could find them," and he winked.

"They didn't try to follow you?" Ted queried.

"Well, no," Curly agreed, "they didn't. You see, I chucked their boots in a fast-flowing stream. It didn't worry me. Trici, the woman in charge of these youngsters, told me the name of Dravadavitch stunk for miles—he was a murderer, robbed churches, etc. . . . so I thought if he had to do a bit of hopping it might do him a power of good."

Under cover of darkness that night the children were embarked on the E-boat. Four of the women came with them, but Trici and another woman refused to travel to Italy. They stayed behind with the Partisans, thankfully accepting British tommy-guns and magazines of spare ammunition. They still had a job to do—to help clear the Germans out of Yugoslavia.

Twenty-six hours later the E-boat, flying a white ensign which the commander of the destroyer had loaned to Ted, limped into Bari harbour. She was not a pretty picture. Her midships was almost gutted by fire, and she resembled a pepper-pot with the number of bullet holes in her hull and upper works.

To a jeering inquiry from a seaman on a tanker Sam Foster yelled:

"She's okay, brother. She's been where you'll probably never go . . . across there where the Jerries shoot on sight. And look at our passengers! They think she's first class."

The hollow-cheeked children stared in amazement at everything about the busy harbour, and many of them insisted on kissing the Fighting Four before being carried off to waiting ambulances. They thought the E-boat was a wonderful ship, and one of them who spoke a little English had christened her H.M.S. *Rescue*.

When Ted Harris had reported to his headquarters he came back with a chit which would enable him and his three friends to get a complete change of clothing, and a bath.

"I don't suppose you'll be shaving, China, will you?" Ted suggested, no sign of a smile on his face.

"Shaving!" China Brown snarled, lifting a hand to his upper lip, masked by a patch of dirty plaster. "Who the heck could shave with a lip like this?"

"It was just a thought," Ted chuckled, winking at Sam Foster and Curly Bates. "I just wondered whether it might be an opportunity for you to grow one of those big, handlebar moustaches the RAF boys wear. You might join the Air Force, once you get a proper bit of face fungus on your upper lip. I think we could manage better if there were only three of us. It'd . . . okay, clot, I was only joking," he added hurriedly, "I was only joking."

He linked an arm in China's and swung off the street to where a big sign denoted baths for army personnel. As they stood under the showers, with soap suds washing down their legs Sam Foster called across:

"What's the first move from here, Sarge?"

"Well, there's a Naval officer promised me a long, long drink," Ted called back.

"I'm going to the hospital, to see how Mike is," Sam spluttered, spitting out soapy water. "I took a big liking to that youngster."

Which was one reason why, when clean, shaved, and spruced up in fresh uniforms, the Fighting Four walked down the road to the hospital to visit a big-hearted youngster from the mountains of Yugoslavia. Ted delighted Michaelovitch by telling him some of the things the Fighting Four had done, and finished up with a promise:

"When you are big enough, Mike, you can join us . . . and we'll change our name from the Fighting Four to the Fighting Four-and-a-half!"

THE END